Books by Jeff Sadler
in the Linford Western Library:

MATAMOROS MISSION

SOLEDAD

When Soledad rode into Tylerville to sell her horses she hadn't counted on staying long. But after she met Alice Treharne and sided her in a crooked card game, it seemed friendly to tag along. By the time Soledad discovered the horse deal was also crooked she was in jail waiting to be hanged. Alice didn't aim to let her die, but danger surrounded them and their enemies were ready to kill. Only low cunning and deadly skills would suffice!

Warwickshire County Council

MOBILE LIBRARY SERVICE

Ale.

Chandos

Wattons

2 4 SEP 2015

1 2 FEB 2016

3 NOV 2016

-3 FEB 2017

1 6 MAY 2019

2 4 JUL 2017

This item is to be returned or renewed before the latest date above. It may be borrowed for a further period if not in demand. **To renew your books:**

- **Phone the 24/7 Renewal Line 01926 499273 or**
- **Visit www.warwickshire.gov.uk/libraries**

Discover ● Imagine● Learn ● *with libraries*

£B

**Warwickshire** County Council

Working for Warwickshire

0134237457

JEFF SADLER

◆

SOLEDAD

Complete and Unabridged

LINFORD
Leicester

First published in Great Britain in 1999 by
Robert Hale Limited
London

First Linford Edition
published 2000
by arrangement with
Robert Hale Limited
London

British Library CIP Data

Sadler, Jeff
 Soledad.—Large print ed.—
 Linford western library
 1. Western stories
 2. Large type books
 I. Title
 823.9'14 [F]

 ISBN 0–7089–5668–8

Published by
F. A. Thorpe (Publishing) Ltd.
Anstey, Leicestershire

Set by Words & Graphics Ltd.
Anstey, Leicestershire
Printed and bound in Great Britain by
T. J. International Ltd., Padstow, Cornwall

This book is printed on acid-free paper

1

They say fast introductions are the best, so maybe I shouldn't complain. That was what I had in Tylerville, and no mistake. I'd barely been in town long enough to stable my roan and get the other horses corralled ready for the buyer when I met up with Vaughan Burrell. The way it happened was a touch faster than I'd have liked. And at that, it was his horse introduced itself the first.

Take my advice, never step off the walk when the sun's in your eyes. Looking back on it now I figure I've made smarter moves in my time, but right then the street seemed quiet enough. Sun was so fierce you could have fried yourself an egg out there in the middle of Front Street if you had a mind, though judging from the fly-blown heaps the dogs and horses left

1

behind I wouldn't have cared to try it. The wood that fronted the buildings was warped and weathered, old paint flaking and bubbling in the heat. But for the lone mongrel hound that lay and scratched himself for fleas in the shade of the walk, nothing out there stirred a stump. The sunlight hit me hard between the eyes as I came down off the boardwalk and I tugged my hat-brim lower, squinting in the glare as I headed for Finn Mahoney's place across the street.

That's when I heard the yelling from further along the walk, and the rattle of hooves coming on at a fast lick for where I was planted.

The horse was a big bay gelding, mighty handsome beast from what I could make of him. Right now he was flying at me so fast he looked like he'd just been shot out of a piece of US Army field artillery, his eyes and nostrils wide and the spray lathering his lips. He was one scared horse all right, but that wasn't about to stop him trampling me flatter than a busted flush if I didn't step aside. Way down the street behind him I could see some other fellers chasing after, but they none of them had a hope of catching him up. If it hadn't been for the halter-rope that the critter trailed after him in the dirt, neither would I.

I must have figured all of this a way quicker than it takes to tell. Leastways, I pitched myself out of his track as he came up like a wall in front, and flipped the hat from my head in the same half-second. It dropped over his eyes and he checked and stumbled, catching a foot in the rope. I got both hands to the rawhide as he stepped out of it, and hauled back with my heels dug in the ground. The bay horse shook off my hat and blew down his nose fierce as a Union Pacific locomotive, setting off again. That feller was so scared and strong he tugged me clean off my feet, and I hit the dirt of Front Street harder than I'd have liked for comfort. The ground was rutted and holed, burned hard as a bone. It was like hitting a cast-iron washboard, and I felt the breath go whooshing out of me as I landed. Lucky for me the gelding had slowed by then, and I scrambled up before he got any further, hauling him down to a shying, frightened walk. Once I got my wind back, I started talking.

'Take it easy, big feller,' I told him. I walked to him, gathering up the rope. 'Ain't nobody gonna hurt you now.'

He snorted at me a couple of times, and made like he'd rear up on his hind legs, but I kept on talking and he thought better of it. After a while he quit shying and just stood and trembled, the sweat shining smooth on his flanks as I patted and gentled him down. I had him all but quieted when the first of the chasing bunch showed up.

'So you caught him, huh?' the *hombre* said. He started in for the horse, lifting the rawhide quirt he carried. 'Thought you'd run from me, did you? Sure as hell got you now, you son of a bitch!'

Now I know God didn't make us all alike, and I know none of us is perfect neither, but I have to say it: he was as ugly and mean-looking a cuss as ever gave displeasure to the eye. The bay horse saw things the same way, I reckon. He took one look and set off to shying and tugging on the rope, shaking as he tried to break loose. I kept a grip on the halter and moved across, coming between him and the feller with the whip.

'Just leave him be, mister,' I told him. 'You already got him scared half to death. Use that thing an' he'll take off runnin' again.'

'That's my hoss, goddammit!' The *hombre* sounded as mean as he looked. He tried to get around me and I moved with him, stepping out ahead. Seeing I wasn't about to let him by he pulled up short, looking me over. Close up, he didn't improve any. He was no taller than me, but nearly twice as wide, with a heavy thick-set build that put me in mind of an adobe privy I saw once outside Laredo. His hands were big and red as ham hocks, and his face looked like a mule had kicked it. The nose was busted flat, splayed out across his cheeks, and a black stubble of beard covered everywhere else below the eyes. I didn't care for them, either. They were muddy brown and bloodshot, and the way they were studying me now was none too friendly.

'Maybe so,' I allowed. 'Then again, I just caught him for you, an' I been around horses all my life. Go easy on him, or he'll be trouble later. That's my advice, an' I reckon you oughta take it.'

'Is that right?' He grinned, but there wasn't anything pleasant about it. The teeth he showed were stumpy and yellow-brown and made a fanged hole in the bristle of his face. I caught a waft of his breath and felt my face pucker up as it landed. With breath like he had, you could scour out a skillet, I reckon. 'You about to give him to me, or what?'

'Just as soon as you put down that whip,' I said.

At that his face swelled up the way a toad does when you poke it with a stick. For a while I figured he was going to bust apart, and the way he spluttered and choked you could see it was a sore trial to him to get out the words he was looking for. As it happened, he didn't get the chance to tell me what was on his mind. Instead, another voice spoke from behind him.

'Put down the quirt, Rufe, and let her be,' this one said. 'I'd say she just saved us a deal of trouble.'

As voices went it was pleasant enough, but it had kind of an edge to it that wasn't to be fooled with. Like the *hombre* who used it didn't often take no for an answer. Once Rufe heard it, it worked like a charm. He kind of froze up stiff like he'd just hit a wall, and swallowed down whatever he'd been about to say to me. It took him quite an effort to keep it down, and from the look on his face those words he was eating must have tasted mighty bad, but he did it all the same. The arm that held the quirt brought it down slowly, and for a while all I heard was the fierce sound of his breathing.

'You were supposed to be looking after that horse,' the second feller said. He took a step closer, that same bite in his voice. 'Now pick up the rope and take him back. And don't let me see you raise that whip to him again, you hear?'

'Sure thing, Mr Burrell.' Rufe sounded like he wasn't enjoying any of this, but knew he'd better do like he was told. He held out a hand for the gelding's rope, shooting me a look that would have poisoned most rattlers I've met. 'You gonna let me have him, lady?'

'Long as you treat him right,' I said.

I gave him the halter and he led the horse clear. The critter was still wary of him, and tugged on the rein, but he went along. I watched the pair of them head back along the street, and turned to pick up my hat from the dirt. I was still beating the dust out of my shirt and cord pants when the second *hombre* spoke again.

'Much obliged to you, ma'am,' the feller said. He smiled, stretching out his hand to me. 'That's a valuable beast you saved for us there. Couple of yards further and he could have busted his leg in that halter-rope. Vaughan Burrell's the name, and I'm mighty pleased to meet you.'

'Likewise, Mr Burrell,' I looked him over in the moment I shook his hand and let it go. What I saw seemed to answer pretty well, I thought. Burrell was medium tall and stocky, with a ruddy fresh-coloured face. He was rigged out in range gear, but cut neat and expensive, not what a cowhand would wear. The brown shirt had an arrow embroidered on its breast pocket, the light-grey pants a shade too tight for workaday use, and the necktie and boots were hand-painted and hand-tooled. He made one hell of a difference to Rufe in his sweaty plaid shirt and shotgun chaps, now almost out of sight as he led the gelding back for the stables. This *hombre* had a dollar or two to spare, from the look of him.

'Vaughan Burrell, you say? I reckon you're the feller I come here to meet.'

'You're Soledad? The horse-dealer from Arizona?' Burrell's smile was giving the sun a contest. He studied me closely, blue eyes showing light and pale in his ruddy, weatherbeaten face. 'Well now, this surely is a pleasure.'

Seeing him stand there so neat and sharp made me feel dustier than ever, and I slapped out a cloud of the stuff from my shirt and pants. Looked like I'd been caught in a fist-fight at the flourmill, and that was the truth. As if I hadn't gathered enough dust getting here from Arizona, before the bay came calling.

'I was headed over to Mahoney's when the horse showed up,' I told him. 'Aimed to meet with you there like we

10

agreed. Just got here a mite early, I guess.'

He didn't answer, the smile still in place as he nodded his head. Recalling the other feller, I glanced away down the street, but by now nothing but the fading dust-clouds could be seen.

'That *hombre* yonder, he works for you, that right?'

'Rufe Simmons, you mean?' Burrell shrugged, still beaming like the dawn coming up. If the question bothered him, he sure as hell didn't show it. 'You could say that. He runs errands for me now and again, that kind of thing.' He broke off, seeming to study me a little closer with those pale eyes of his. 'Don't you pay any mind to Rufe, Soledad. His bark is worse than his bite, that's all.'

'You reckon.' My voice came out a mite hotter than intended, I guess. Maybe it was thinking about Rufe, and what he'd have done to the gelding if I hadn't got in the way. 'Fact is, Mr Burrell, I can't stand to see a horse treated bad. It ain't right, an' it ain't

11

good business neither.'

'No way I aim to argue with that.' Burrell was still unfazed, that smile cracking his face. Could be his eyes were a touch colder than they'd been before, then again it might have been nothing of the kind. 'Ain't in my nature to contradict a lady anyhow, Soledad. Tell truth, Rufe Simmons is my responsibility. His folks and mine were friends way back when the two of us were children, and I reckon nobody else around here would take him on. Figure a man oughta show a little Christian charity once in a while, that's the way I see it.'

'From the look of him, you have to be quite a Christian, Mr Burrell,' I said.

That came out shorter than I'd meant it, too. I didn't care for the way those eyes were studying me, running all the way down to my boots and back up again. I knew that women were rare as hen's teeth in Tylerville like they are most places hereabouts, and it ain't often a feller gets to see one close to, least of all one that dresses like a man in shirt and cords. Maybe that was cause enough for a Christian man like Mr Burrell to be looking me over that way, but that don't mean I'm bound to like it. That kind of studying I've seen plenty of times, and when I want it I'll ask. Better believe it.

'Fine. Just fine.' Burrell rubbed his hands together, trying to sound brisker than he'd been before. 'So let's do business, Miss Soledad. You have the horses ready where I can see them?'

'Sure, got 'em corralled out back.' I turned around, starting across the street with him following after. 'All you have to do is look, I guess.'

We recrossed Front Street, both of us with our hats pulled low against the sun. This time, though, I kept an eye open for any sudden moves. Nothing else decided to show and we made it to the corner of the nearest block, heading on down the alley, with its chewed bones and busted tomato cans, for the corrals out back.

Out behind Front Street, the town seemed to drop away altogether, hindward side of the hardware and general stores and the Mex *cantina* giving on to a spavined sprawl of brush windbreaks and lean-to shacks, and after that to nothing at all. Beyond the two pole-fenced corrals, Texas stretched away as far as the eye could see, sagebrush and postoak covering the flats that broke gradually uphill into slopes and gullies and higher yet to the woods on the shoulders of the mountains that made a hard knife-edge on the sky with their sawtooth peaks. Nothing but badland and heat-haze like a quivering bead curtain between sight and the skyline. Crushing heat with not the hint of a breeze, and the sun fierce as burning pitch on your head and shoulders as you stood to take it in. After a while you could hear the stillness thudding like a drum in your head, fit to bust it apart.

'Now you see 'em, Mr Burrell,' I said.

I nodded to where the six horses

circled inside the pole corral, stamping a little in the rising dust and flicking with manes and tails at the hovering flies. I watched the smooth lines of their bodies as they shifted and slid by, gleam of sunlight on their flanks and haunches. Heads flung up at the sound of my voice, their eyes fixing on me, and it was my turn to smile. I've been around a while now, but I reckon there ain't no prettier sight than a bunch of good horses in their prime, just pleased to be the way they are.

'Six topnotch workin' horses,' I told him. 'All of 'em saddle-broke an' ready to go. An' if you reckon you kin pick out a fault in one of 'em, you're surely welcome to try.'

I led him down to the corral and leaned with my elbows on the topmost pole of the fence, whistling the nearest of the bunch. He stepped over and I patted his neck and let him nuzzle while Burrell ducked down to check him over from close quarters. When he straightened up again he nodded his head, satisfied.

'He's fine, sure enough,' the fresh-faced man allowed. He stepped away from the corral fence, eyeing me carefully. 'From here, they all look pretty good to me. All of 'em browns, I see.'

'That's right.' I looked the moving horses over, still smiling, 'Used to be a horsebreaker with the army, one time, Mr Burrell. Nowadays most of my business is with the military, an' they go for solid colour horses. Had me a stud palomino once, but once I sold him, that was all.'

'Uhuh.' Burrell let his glance drift back the way mine had gone. 'They're good stock, from what I can tell of it. What's your price, Miss Soledad?'

'Just like it was before, Mr Burrell,' I told him. 'Reckon you heard it right the first time.'

'Guess so,' He started to smile again, a mite ruefully. 'Seems to me you believe in charging a man top dollar, Miss Soledad?'

'What you got here is first-class bloodstock, Mr Burrell. Ain't askin' you to pay me a cent more than they'd fetch anyplace else.'

He appeared to think it over for a while, and I let him ponder, watching the horses circle inside the corral. After about a half-minute, he nodded.

'Have it your way, lady.' He dug in the inside pocket of his coat and brought out a well-stuffed billfold, began counting out a thick sheaf of greenbacks. 'Reckon I'll take 'em, even at that.'

I held out my hand and let him fill it, totting up the score as the stack of notes grew higher. Crisp wad of fives and tens and twenties, just a little used. They felt genuine enough, all right. I closed my grip over them slowly, maybe a little surprised. I was used to most buyers arguing the pitch a way longer than this. Wasn't usual to have one pay up like today, prompt as you please.

'Got the bill of sale right here, Mr Burrell.' I drew the folded paper from my shirt breast pocket and handed it over. 'You'll find that counts for somethin' in these parts.'

'I don't doubt it.' Burrell studied the paper and stowed it inside his coat, watched as I tucked the dollars safely in the back pocket of my cords. He stretched out a hand to me, the old smile cracking his face again. 'A pleasure to do business with you, Soledad.'

'Goes for me too, Mr Burrell,' I said.

We shook hands and stood a while, both of us waiting for the other to speak.

'That was the business, now how about the pleasure?' Burrell's voice had a bright, forced sound to it. He looked me over, a little more warily than before. 'You care for a drink with me, maybe?'

Another time I might have told him no, but not today. I'd eaten more dust than I cared to remember, and my throat was parched as a fly-blown buffalo hide. And with the bruises I'd taken from Front Street coming back to pain me, I reckoned that a drink was just what I needed.

'Sure, Mr Burrell,' I said. 'I'd like that.'

'That's what I was waiting to hear, Miss Soledad,' he told me.

He turned his back on the horses, heading towards the alley that led on to Front Street, and Mahoney's place. He smiled at me as he went, sweeping an arm forward to beckon me after him. I guess by this time he knew better than to try linking arms or any of that stuff. I followed him through the litter of cans and trash in the alley, checking the wad of dollar bills in my back pocket. I figured I'd done what I came here for, the horses were sold and I had the price I wanted. All the same, there was something about it I didn't care for. Something not quite as it should be. Like a dollar that rings on a bar top, and you know right away it's a fake. Just what it was I couldn't rightly tell, but I knew I didn't like it. Chances were, I wouldn't be any happier once I found out either.

I checked out both sides of Front Street for runaway horses, and followed Burrell, sweating harder in the fierce sunlight.

One thing I knew for sure was, I needed that drink.

2

Finn Mahoney's saloon stood waiting for us at the far side of Front Street. Must have been five or six years now since I'd been in Tylerville, but from what I could see the place hadn't changed overmuch. No fresh paint had gone on the walls, the same flakes peeling from the wood in the heat of the sun, and the panelled doors were battered and worn thin from all the drinkers who'd shoved their way through over the years. Burrell pushed them open and stepped inside, holding the near one back to allow me through. I was alongside him as the pair of us threaded our way past the seated drinkers and gamblers at their tables, and on towards the bar.

Inside, Mahoney's was pretty much as I remembered. The place had nothing much in the way of light, and

21

the windows were shuttered against the heat, but the sun was so strong the glare hit through chinks in the wood everywhere, blades of golden light striking through the heavy shadows and catching the floating specks of dust. Maybe half-a-dozen tables were crammed into the space in front of the bar, and all of them looked to be well filled with miners and gamblers nursing their cards or their glasses of liquor. Finn's was the best saloon in Tylerville, and one of the best in this stretch of Texas. Right here, it was the only place where the whiskey didn't taste of turpentine and wasn't like to send you blind. And if Finn always had a rattler's head nailed to the bottom of the keg to give a taste to the drinks, so what? It was something most saloon-men this side of the Pecos tried sooner or later.

Away to the left an undernourished *hombre* in a derby hat was hammering the tar out of an aged piano that leaned slightly askew on account of one of its legs had started to bow like a cowhand just stepped down from his horse. I couldn't rightly make out what tune he aimed to play once he found it, but he was sure as hell making that piano suffer, and you could hear it plain. Back of him a young Mexican kid was plucking away at his guitar, but it sounded like he was playing something else altogether, and the two tunes didn't fit too well. Might have been 'Red River Valley' and 'Las Mañanitas' if I had to put a name to either one, but I wouldn't want you to take my word for it.

We got by them, too, and bellied up against the pine bar that ran half the width of the saloon. The wood of the bar top was gouged and splintered, dark with beer and whiskey stains, but it sure looked welcome to me. Just like the bottles on the shelves behind.

'So what'll it be, gents?' Finn Mahoney asked.

He loomed up out of the shadows on the right and up to the bar on its far side, setting both hands on the wooden surface and looking us over. Once he set eyes on me I could see the grin steal across his face.

'Make it a beer this time, Finn,' I told him.

'Soledad! If that don't beat all!' Finn sounded as pleased as he looked. He was short and heavyset, muscles hard as wood knots under the old hickory shirt, and the hands on the bar top were calloused and tough. He had broad, strong Negro features and his skin was a deep-brown shade, but Finn's hair was red like rusty iron and he had freckles and light-green eyes that didn't look away. The way I heard it, Finn's mother had been a runaway slave and his old man an Irish dirt farmer, and the two of them had met up twenty-some years ago back in Arkansas. Not that it was any of my business, nor anyone else's come to that. What counted right now was he was pleased to see me. 'Sure is good to see you, and that's a fact.'

24

'Good to see you too, Finn,' I grinned back, watching as he filled the glass and slid it over. After the fierce heat outside, its touch was cool to my hand as it closed around the drink. 'Business still good from the look of it, I reckon.'

'Mine's a whiskey, Finn,' Vaughan Burrell said.

He sounded kind of impatient, that edge to his voice I'd heard once before, and when I glanced across to him I saw he wasn't smiling either. Finn heard that edge in it, too, and lost some of his grin for an instant.

'Sure thing, Mr Burrell.' He reached for the shelf behind him, turned to set up the bottle and glass. 'Coming right up.'

Burrell stayed watching him as he poured the drink. He still didn't smile. I figured it was nothing to do with me and took a sip at the beer, feeling the cool liquid thin out the dust in my throat. Finn had an old gilt-framed mirror hung back of the bar, that I hadn't seen the last time I called. From the way the gilt had begun to wear off the frame, and the smears that coated it you could tell it was kind of old, but a feller might still see his face in it if he had a mind. I studied my reflection in the glass while Finn was pouring Burrell's whiskey. What I saw there was just about what I'd expected. The woman staring back at me was slim and on the tall side for a female, narrow-hipped maybe but with all the curves in the right places. She was rigged in a denim shirt and cord pants worn outside a pair of down-at-heel boots, a wide-brim Stetson shading her face. Whole outfit was coated white with dust, and sweat cut runnels in the dirt on her cheeks. Her face was a touch darker than most, but smooth and without any smallpox scars. Wouldn't call her a beauty, but I reckon I've seen plenty worse in my time. I shook the hair back out of my eyes and watched her do the same, the thick strands gleaming as they fell back on to her

shoulders. Black, coarse hair that always gave the shears a hard time. Indian hair, they call it. But with folks like I had, what else would it be?

I'd left the mirror to itself, and was halfway through sinking my beer, when Finn Mahoney's voice shook me out of the dream I'd dropped into.

'We get by, I guess,' the saloonman murmured. He ignored Burrell for the moment, his green eyes pale in the dark face as he glanced my way again. 'How come you're in Tylerville, Soledad?'

'Sellin' horses, what else?' I nod across to where Burrell swigged o whiskey, stony featured. 'Just myself a little *dinero* out of Mr here; he has six of my best horses. Seems like we're be happy with the deal.'

'Is that right?' The red sound like he was too ple he heard. 'Always welcor you know that.'

'Sure I do,' I told h drinkin' anywhere els

That got a smile from him, at least. He might have said something else to me then, but Vaughan Burrell drained his glass and eased away from the bar, and now he was looking my way.

'That hit the spot, all right,' Burrell breathed out contentedly. All at once, he'd regained his smile. 'Finish your beer, Miss Soledad. Some folks here I'd like you to meet.'

He stepped closer in, one thumb hooked into his belt as the other indicated a group of *hombres* at one of the nearer tables. Half-turning with him, I caught Finn Mahoney's eye. The saloon-keeper said nothing, but it seemed to me those eyes might just be trying to warn me about something. Maybe I should have read his message a le better, but that's the way life is. ne you win, and some you lose.

ight over here,' Vaughan Burrell

moved away from the bar, ng for the seated group. I took a w at the beer before I offered to

28

follow, savouring the last of that welcome chill as it made its way down. By the time I caught up with him again he was at the table and waiting for me, beckoning me closer as the others shifted in their chairs to look my way. I read the eyes of every man in that bunch around the table, and didn't care for what I found there. And, but for Burrell, not a one of them cracked a smile. Last time I met their kind of reception I was riding past a cluster of buzzards on the carcass of a mule. These *hombres* seemed about as friendly.

Worse yet, one of them was Rufe Simmons, and he looked just as ugly and mean the second time around.

'Gents, meet my friend Miss Soledad,' the fresh-faced man was saying. 'She's just sold me some mighty expensive saddle-horses.' He beamed at his own joke, the way some of them Tombstone comedians do when they're fighting to get a laugh. 'Soledad, meet my business associates — Jake Brocklehurst, Kirk Ashman.' Catching the scowl from his burly, bearded sidekick he grinned a little tighter. 'Rufe, here, you already met, I reckon.'

'Guess so.' I nodded to the thick-set *hombre*, trying not to take too much of the poison in his gaze. Right now it seemed he was struggling to fit himself into the rickety chair that didn't suit his bulk any more than it would a grizzly bear. Simmons eased his lips back from his teeth, the nearest he came to smiling. To me, it looked like he was fixing to bite me, and it wasn't any too pleasant. '*Buenas dias*, Mr Brocklehurst, Mr Ashman.'

They grinned at that, leaning halfway from their chairs to shake hands. All the while their eyes raked me over, working out the chances. Ashman was gangling and tall as a sprouting weed, with buck teeth and wide, staring eyes. His tow hair stuck out from under his hat like ragged straw. More than you could say for Brocklehurst, an undersized little feller in a worn leather vest. He took off his hat as we shook, and I saw his head gleam with the move, pink and bald through thinning strands of hair.

'Sure is a pleasure, lady,' Brocklehurst said. He made to smile, but the eyes stayed watchful and hard. Alongside him Ashman said nothing, fixing me with that wide-eyed stare. Burrell appeared not to notice, nodding towards the last man at the table.

'Meet Lucas Hildreth,' Burrell said. 'He's dentist and undertaker here in Tylerville.'

'Charmed, I'm sure.' Hildreth leered at me like a lobo wolf, reaching out a hand. He was a thin, dried-up-looking cuss with a face that was mostly grin and wrinkles, fixed around a bitten cigar stump in the corner of his mouth. He wore an old clawhammer coat and a flat-crowned black hat, and I had to admit he was dressed for the part.

'Ain't too often we have a lady honour us this way, Miss Soledad.'

'Mister Hildreth.' I shook hands,

leaning across the table. Hildreth's handshake was firm enough, but I was glad when he let go his grip. Couldn't help but think of those hands setting the lid down on some poor jasper whose time had run out, and then reaching to fix the nails. 'Guess it's good to be here too, after a long ride.'

'Take a seat, Soledad.' Burrell smiled easily, pulling out an old ladderback from next to him. At a nod from him Ashman and Brocklehurst got up hurriedly, leaving their own chairs empty. 'We were about to take a hand at cards, but as it happens we're a couple of players short. Jake and Kirk here have business to attend to, and it can't wait. Isn't that right, boys?'

'Sure, Mr Burrell.' Brocklehurst crammed the hat on his shiny head, his face sulky as a slapped kid. Beside him the buck-toothed feller, Ashman, looked almost as sore. The little man nodded to me, trying not to show it. 'Been nice meetin' you, lady.'

He touched a scowling Ashman on

the sleeve, and the pair of them turned, moving for the doors. I was still watching them go when I heard the other voice.

'I'll have a glass of lemonade, if you please,' the woman said.

She spoke from behind us, up by the bar. Where she sprang from I'll never know, but there she was all the same. When I turned my head I saw her plain. She was small and slight, wearing a sunbonnet and an old grey dress that reached almost to the floor. From here I couldn't see her face as her back was to us, but Finn Mahoney could, and one look at him was all I needed. If he'd been pleased to see me, this one left him dumbstruck. It ain't often Finn runs short on words, but I reckon it must have been close on a minute before he found his voice.

'Lemonade.' Finn turned the word around kind of thoughtful. He didn't get to use it often, after all. 'Whatever you say, lady. Lemonade it is, comin' up.'

Seemed like the whole room went quiet at that. Even the feller in the derby quit torturing the piano to look sideways at what he heard, and the Mexican kid eased off from strumming for a while to listen in. The woman at the bar paid them and us no mind at all, waiting while Finn struggled among the lower shelves before coming back with a bottle that looked like it had seen better days. She stayed there, standing stiff as a sentry, watching him dust off the worst of the cobwebs and break out the glass. Once the drink was poured she ducked her head, flipping a coin on the bar top.

'Most refreshing,' the woman said. She sipped the lemonade, nodding slowly. 'I thank you, barman.'

Finn didn't say a thing. It seemed like it was all he could do to breathe.

'Soledad.' That was Vaughan Burrell, and he sounded impatient. 'Like I said, we were about to play a hand. You care to join us, maybe?'

I turned back to him as he spoke, and

34

caught the three of them looking my way. I could have been wrong, maybe, but to me all three men Burrell, Rufe Simmons and the undertaker, Hildreth — had the same kind of glint in their eye. The kind of shine a hawk's eye gets, just before it sets to swoop.

'Well now, Mr Burrell.' I was none too sure about this, and it showed in my voice. 'I just got here, and I reckon I've seen as much action as I need, out on the street. Tell truth, I could use a hot bath and some shut-eye, if it's all the same to you.'

It wasn't as if I was fooling him, neither. Once I settled into that chair I started to feel those bruises I'd taken on Front Street, just as if that bay horse had come back and kicked me in the ribs himself. Then again, I could tell from the looks I got that it wasn't all the same to them. Seemed they were real keen for me to stay.

'Just a little wager, that's all.' Burrell's smile was back again. Trouble was, it had no more warmth to it than those icy-pale eyes of his. 'Nothing much, just a hand or so between friends. Like Lucas here says, isn't often a lady stops by here.'

'That's right, Miss Soledad.' Hildreth grinned around the cigar stub, his dark eyes sunk deep in the wrinkles all around. 'We'd surely appreciate it.'

Rufe Simmons said nothing, just sat and watched me, hard and mean as ever. Like he was waiting for me to get up and run.

Now I saw the noose hung out for me, sure enough. You might even say I could feel the hemp strands around my neck. Trouble was, the knowing came a way too late. Across the table, Hildreth grinned tighter and broke out a pack of cards, riffling them through like he'd had plenty of practice. I was still working out what to say when a light footstep sounded on the dirt floor behind me, and I looked up to see the woman standing there, the glass of lemonade still clutched in her hand.

'I see you gentlemen are about to take cards,' she said.

It was a strange way of speaking she had. Not the way folks talked in Tylerville, or anywhere else I'd been. Kind of tight and clipped, but some hint of brogue in it that I'd never heard before. Right now I let it pass, studying her a little closer. She had a neat, womanly figure that filled the drab grey dress a way better than it deserved. Framed inside the big sunbonnet her face seemed smaller than it was, smooth and rosy pink, with wide blue eyes and neat golden curls peeping out either side. So small and dainty she might have been a china doll, almost, but what I saw told me she was real enough. No doubt about it, she was mighty pretty, and I reckon if I'd been a man I might just have been as dumbstruck as Finn Mahoney and everybody else. I reckon she knew it, too.

At the sound of her voice the three of them looked up, and I swear their eyes lit up like fire-crackers on the Fourth of July.

'Why, good afternoon, ma'am,' Vaughan Burrell said. The hat was clear of his head quicker than you could snap a whip. 'This is a pleasure, and no mistake.'

'You're too kind, I'm sure,' she smiled back at him, scanning the rest of us at the table. 'I don't believe we've been introduced. My name is Alice Treharne, I'm up here from St Louis.'

'Vaughan Burrell, ma'am. Mighty pleased to make your acquaintance.' The fresh-faced *hombre* indicated the others. 'My business associates, Lucas Hildreth, Rufe Simmons. And this here is Miss Soledad, she's in town to sell her horses.'

'Miss Soledad.' Alice Treharne stretched out her hand, and we shook.

'Good to know you, ma'am,' I told her. Although her hand was small, I couldn't help but notice it had one hell of a grip.

'Oh, come now.' Seemed like those wide blue eyes mocked at me. 'Alice will do.'

'If you say so, Alice,' I said.

'You take an interest in cards, ma'am?' Lucas Hildreth asked. He flicked through the deck in front of him, eyes fixed on her as he bit on the cigar.

'Why, yes, Mr Hildreth. As a bystander, of course.' Alice blushed prettily, her rosy cheeks showing their dimples. 'I find games of chance fascinating, don't you?'

'Most assuredly, ma'am.' Hildreth's grin had gone tight and mean around the stump of his cigar, those black birdy eyes of his raking her over. 'Maybe you'd like to join us, take in a hand or so.' He nodded across to me, flipping the deck. 'As you see, we already have one lady in the game.'

'Just a minute now,' I started. 'I ain't never said I was playin'.'

From the corner of my eye I caught Rufe Simmons looking my way, and if looks could have killed I'd have been on my way to Heaven or some-place warmer. I stayed quiet. Alice, though, appeared to have missed the whole thing.

'Well now, Mr Hildreth.' She blushed a deeper shade, hanging her head. 'You gentlemen must understand I have never played this kind of game — for money, I mean. Just a hand of gin rummy with my dear departed father now and again, God rest him.' She paused, half-turning to dab a scented handkerchief to her eyes for a moment. 'A fine man, gentlemen. There are times when I feel his loss, I'm afraid.'

'I'm sure he'd be proud to see his daughter right now,' Burrell offered. For all his smiling, I got the feeling he was running out of patience. 'Say you'll join us, ma'am. A harmless wager, a game of chance as you put it. What could be wrong with that?'

Alice thought about that, taking a careful sip of the lemonade left in her glass. After a while she turned and nodded, her smile returning.

'I believe you have convinced me, Mr Burrell.' She moved forward, settling into the empty seat he drew out for her and smoothing out her thread-bare gown. Alice laid both hands in her lap and beamed at everyone around the table. 'You'll have to explain to me how the game is played. I can't say that I'm familiar with wagers of this kind.'

'Don't you worry, ma'am. We'll show you how,' Burrell told her. He glanced across to me, his tone a mite less friendly than before. 'Made up your mind, Miss Soledad?'

'If Alice here is game, I reckon I'll play along,' I said.

'Then that's settled.' Hildreth's voice grew brisk and businesslike, faster than Burrell had pulled off his hat. He turned to the seated figure of Alice, giving her the full benefit of his alligator grin. 'The game's poker, ma'am. It involves luck, and bluff, and perhaps a little skill also. First of all, though, each player must be prepared to put up a

41

stake, which contributes to what we call the pot.'

'You are speaking of money, I take it?' Alice eyed him real serious, like he was some kind of teacher and she was eager to learn. 'I have a hundred dollars with me, Mr Hildreth, all I have left in the world. It was a gift from my dear papa, before he passed on.' She broke off, seeming to collect herself for a moment, and dug into the tiny reticule she carried, bringing out a sheaf of dollar bills that she laid on the table in front of her. 'It's the only money I have to offer, I'm afraid.'

'That'll do just fine,' Hildreth told her, and the other two nodded along with him.

I sat there listening as he explained to Alice how a poker game was played, and the way they worked out who won and who lost. I didn't care for it one bit, I can tell you. Watching this little trusting doll of a woman being talked into losing her money by a shark like Hildreth was like watching a sheep smile while the wolves chew it over. I guess I had some idea that if I sat tight and played along I might pitch in to help her once it started to get tough. Not that I was too sure how we'd fare against a bully-boy like Rufe Simmons. Horses I can manage any time; grizzly bears are a mite too rich for my blood, I reckon.

'So, let's play,' Vaughan Burrell said. He took the cards from Hildreth, and started dealing. Pretty soon all five of us held our hand, and the game was on.

From the time Burrell had asked me to play I'd the feeling there was something not quite right about this game. I figured, too, that the rules that Hildreth had been explaining to Alice might not be the only ones they used. It didn't take me long to work out I'd hit the mark. After the first few hands Hildreth was starting to win heavy, and the dollars and the coins were piling up in front of him. Most of Alice's money was in there, and more than half the *dinero* Burrell had paid me for the

43

horses. Worse yet, I could see that was the way it was going to be for the rest of the evening. Somehow the little undertaker in his clawhammer coat seemed to keep finding himself with the best cards in the house. Funny, ain't it?

'Last round, folks!' Hildreth called. He cracked that 'gator grin, his wrinkled face puckering up so tight his eyes all but disappeared in the folds. 'Seems like it's my lucky day, don't it?'

'Sure does,' I muttered. By now, I couldn't rightly claim to be in a charitable mood. Back of us towards the bar the piano-player was pounding away, the Mex kid doing his best to keep up. It might have been 'Buffalo Gals' they were murdering this time around, but it was hard to tell. Wasn't 'The Star-Spangled Banner,' that's for sure. I looked across to Alice, who was almost cleaned out, and pushed half the dollars I had left over to her. Why did I do it? You tell me, feller. Maybe I couldn't stand to see her lose everything. Then again, maybe it was just a feeling.

'Call him, girl,' I told her. 'You got enough there to up the ante. Time we saw what he's been hidin'.'

She eyed me kind of strange at first, like she wasn't too sure what it was I had in mind. Then Alice smiled like the sun coming out, and I knew I'd done right.

'You're too kind, Miss Soledad,' Alice said. She turned back to Hildreth and the other two, those baby-blue eyes suddenly sharp and watchful. 'I'm ready, gentlemen.'

'Showdown.' Hildreth's grin had turned a little edgy. 'Five hundred here says I get to see your hands. How about you, Burrell?'

'Not me; I fold.' The fresh-faced man shrugged ruefully. 'You got too much for me, I reckon.'

'Same goes for me,' Rufe Simmons' voice rumbled, deep in his chest. 'I fold.'

'And me.' I slapped down the cards, scanning their useless faces on the table top. I'd been hoping for a straight, but I was still a card away at the finish. Besides, I had the feeling even if it had come along, a straight wouldn't have been enough.

'That leaves just you, ma'am.' Hildreth's deep-set eyes fixed on Alice, waiting. 'You about to show us your hand now?'

'After you, Mr Hildreth.' Alice smiled politely, studying her hand. She nodded to the money I'd pushed her way. 'I have seven hundred here that covers your bet and raises the stake. Perhaps you'd like to let us see what you're holding.'

I felt the shock of the words as they hit the three *hombres* around the table, caught the quick-fire glances they sent each other, and it was all I could do not to laugh out loud.

'If you insist, ma'am.' Lucas Hildreth bit the words out through his teeth, the 'gator grin wiped from his face. Either side of him, Burrell and Simmons had also quit smiling. The *hombre* in the clawhammer coat set down his cards, slow and steady, and glanced up like he'd already won. 'Full house, Mrs Treharne. I'd say that was a winning hand, all right.'

'We shall see, Mr Hildreth,' Alice beamed at him, laying out her cards in turn. 'I seem to be holding four kings, do I not? What is that called, I wonder.'

'Four of a kind, Alice,' I told her. 'And it beats his hand, and everyone else's.'

'Really? What a wonderful surprise.' She eyed the three scowling *hombres* around the table, bowing her pretty blonde head to each in turn. 'Well, it seems I win the game, gentlemen. Thank you for a most exhilarating contest. If you'll excuse me now, I'll collect my winnings and bid you good-day. I must confess I'm a little tired.'

She leaned forward across the table, scooping the wads of dollars and gold and silver coin towards her as Hildreth and his pals sat staring like they'd all been turned to stone. From the looks on their faces, though, I could tell it wasn't about to stay that way. I eased my chair back slowly, getting ready for trouble.

'You just cheated there, lady!' Rufe Simmons said.

He was the first of them to move, and for a feller his size he moved mighty fast. Alice had barely gathered the winnings her side of the table when he leaned sideways quicker than a rattler strikes, grabbing her wrist and pulling her back down into the chair. From the sharp gasp she gave I knew the son of a bitch was hurting her, and figured I wasn't about to sit and watch. I'd kicked my own chair backwards and started to my feet when I heard Finn Mahoney call out from behind the bar.

'You let, go of her, Simmons!' the saloonman shouted. His voice was so loud it rang clear through the place.

'Do it now, or by God I'm gonna bust your head!'

Everybody quit talking with the noise of that shout, and even the piano-player and his friend left off butchering whatever tune it was they had in mind. I can't say I ever heard a saloon so quiet before in my whole life. When Simmons heard Finn yell he paused halfway through dragging Alice out of her seat, easing his grip a touch so that she slumped in the chair. The thick-set, bearded *hombre* turned his head slowly, looking back to the man at the bar. Finn glared right back at him, his eyes like green glass splinters. He was holding the long-handled hammer they used to knock the bungs into the kegs, and it looked like he was all set to use it right now.

'You talkin' to me, feller?' Simmons wanted to know. As he spoke his hand went reaching for the heavy pistol that jutted butt-forwards from his belt. Finn caught the move, and nodded.

'You heard me, Simmons,' the

redhead told him. 'Touch her again, I'm comin' after you. An' don't go threatenin' me with that cannon you're totin'. You couldn't hit a bull buffalo in the ass if they gave you the month to do it!'

He tapped the hammer on the bar top and Simmons' face swelled up dark and red. He was ready to haul the gun when Vaughan Burrell cut in.

'Do like he says, Rufe,' Burrell said. He'd found that cold edge to his voice again, and it hit like a winter wind. 'Let her go, you hear?'

Simmons didn't like what he heard. He glowered at Finn, and then at Burrell, but he knuckled under just the same. He loosened his grip on Alice's wrist and she gasped again, rubbing the bruised flesh as she glared around the table.

'Really, Mr Simmons! You forget yourself!' She got to her feet, struggling to pile her winnings together. 'I believe it's time I left here, gentlemen. Cards clearly do not improve your temper.'

'Let me help you there, Alice,' I said.

I eased my chair out of the way, and unhitched the bandanna from my neck. She watched while I gathered up the dollar bills and coins inside it, and tied the ends together. Once I was done, I handed it over.

'Why thank you, Miss Soledad.' She smiled, but not too wide, watching me carefully with those blue eyes of hers. 'I daresay I shall manage now.'

She picked up the bandanna and started for the door. I went along with her, moving as slowly as I dared. Behind us some of the drinkers began their talk again, and the music-murderers got back to business. Could have been 'Streets of Laredo', or just about anything else you care to name. Sure as hell sounded terrible, whatever it was.

Behind us came a sudden yell, and the noise of men kicking over chairs and ducking under tables. After it, I heard Rufe Simmons' voice.

'Just stay right where you're at, you bitches!' the bearded *hombre* shouted.

51

Alice and me turned our heads, and found ourselves looking down the business end of the pistol he was holding. Simmons had hauled the gun, and now he had the hammer drawn halfway back. Always a dangerous thing to do, I reckon, especially if you were our side of the gun.

'You ain't a-walkin' out of here, damn it!' Simmons' face was so red and swollen he was like to bust wide open. I could see the spittle flecking his black beard, and knew he was past arguing with by now. 'That's our money you got, you cheatin' whore!'

At that it dropped real quiet, like someone had sworn in church, and Finn Mahoney came lunging around the bar with the bung-hammer lifted for action. When he saw how Simmons held the gun on us the saloonman pulled up short, simmering like a skillet on a griddle.

'Rufe.' Vaughan Burrell's voice came cold enough for snow. 'Rufe, don't be a goddamn' fool. 'Put up the pistol, and let them be.'

'That's right, Rufe.' Hildreth sounded scared for once, eyeing the raised pistol. 'No call for unpleasantness, surely.'

'Let's go, Alice,' I said. As she turned her back on the gun, I glanced to Simmons. 'Sure, Rufe. Go right ahead,' I told him. I held my voice as steady as I could. Not that it was easy, with the pistol waggling in my direction at half cock and a mean, angry son behind it. 'Shoot two women in the back, why don't you? That's gonna look wonderful, ain't it? Quite the gunslinger you'll be, after that. Seems to me you best sit and take your medicine, 'cause we're leavin' now.'

I nodded across to Alice, and we both set off towards the doors again. We hadn't gone more than four or five steps when Simmons called out once more. This time I knew he wasn't fooling.

'Stay put, goddamn it!' Simmons yelled.

Call me an Indian if you like, but I

reckon I sensed it coming before the words got to us. I threw myself headlong into Alice and the pair of us were flat on that dirt floor as the pistol blasted fit to wake the dead. The noise swelled up inside the saloon like somebody had fired a shotgun into a barrel, and we were in it. For a couple of seconds, it felt like my eardrums were about to burst. Then I scrambled up on my hands and knees in time to see Finn Mahoney slam into Simmons and knock him out of his chair. The two men went down in a mill of fists and elbows and knees, rolling around as they battled to do each other some serious damage. I got up as they struggled from the ground, still grappling for a hold.

'Get away from him, Finn!' I shouted.

Burrell and Hildreth were yelling too, but neither of the struggling men paid them or me any mind. Finn got his hammer-arm free and got in a slugging blow to the hand that held the gun, and

Simmons howled, letting the pistol drop. Same time it fell, he broke loose from the saloonman and swung from the ground up with his other fist. That punch would have mown hay in three states, I reckon, if it hadn't caught Finn Mahoney flush on the jaw. The thud as it landed made me shiver, and I saw Finn's eyes glaze over before he hit the floor. He lay sprawled out, gazing at the ceiling of his saloon like he'd just seen it for the first time, and was taking a real close interest in the place.

The pistol skittered towards me along the dirt floor, and Simmons came ploughing after it like a grizzly with his butt afire. I got my foot to it before he could reach, kicking the gun backwards for the doorway. I heard it clatter on the wood behind me, and dipped a hand quickly into the right pocket of my cords, where my own weapon nestled in the pocket holster. I had the pistol out and clear in one smooth move, and it lined up on Rufe Simmons between those muddy eyes as he scrambled on all fours after a gun that wasn't there.

'This here is a Colt .41 pocket model, Mr Simmons,' I told him. I slipped my thumb gently over the hammer the instant I spoke. 'Don't weigh like the pistol you got, an' it don't bust my wrist when it shoots, but it kills mighty dead when you're stood this close. Now on your feet, an' walk back for that table. An' make sure both them hands are lifted.'

I waited for that to sink in, keeping the gun levelled at his head. First few seconds all he could do was stare at me like he'd been slugged by a rock. After that he began to steam a little, and mutter at me through his teeth. Once he saw I wasn't about to oblige him any, he got up and backed away, both hands high above his head. Meeting the poisonous look he gave me, I was kind of happy to be holding the gun.

'Nobody likes a sore loser,' I said. I scanned the other gaping faces in the room, and fixed on Burrell and Hildreth, who now stood close beside their bearded friend looking sorely mistreated. 'Was I you, fellers, I wouldn't say too much about cheatin' at cards. I seen plenty of crimps in your hand, Hildreth, an' all them little signs Rufe here's been givin' you. You *hombres* aimed to get back the *dinero* you paid me for my horses, an' fleece Alice here into the bargain. Well, it didn't work, an' you lost out.'

Over by the table Finn Mahoney groaned and shook his head, returning to life. He'd be lucky if he didn't have a busted jaw, with the punch he'd collected from Simmons. Any other time I'd have stuck around and made sure he was all right, I guess. Right now, I was more interested in getting out of here in one piece.

'This isn't over, Soledad,' Vaughan Burrell told me. His voice was bleak and bitter as a blue norther in hill country, cold enough to make me catch my breath. He hadn't moved from where he stood beside the glowering Rufe Simmons, but that pale-eyed stare of his fixed on me like he aimed to look all the way through me. 'One way or another, you'll be hearing from us again, and soon.'

'If you say so, Mr Burrell.' I backed for the door where Alice waited, clutching the bandanna that held her winnings. Seemed like she didn't intend moving until, I joined her there. 'For now, though, it's *adios*, I reckon. An' don't come lookin' once we're gone.'

'I have to say you disappoint me, Soledad,' he said.

'You too, Mr Burrell,' I told him.

I was up by the doorway now, my back to the wall. The fallen pistol knocked against my foot and I bent to gather it left-handed from the ground, making sure my own .41 stayed fixed on Simmons. As the dumbest *hombre* in the place, he was the likeliest to make a move. Neither Burrell nor Hildreth appeared to be armed, and nobody else was about to buy in on their account. As it happened, Simmons decided to be smart for once, and none of them gave me any trouble.

'That's all,' I said. I straightened up with a gun in either hand, and nodded across to Alice, who still stood waiting. 'Reckon we can go now, Alice.'

She didn't say anything, just turned and pushed out through the doors and on to the walk. I backed out after her, slowly. None of the drinkers made a move to stop me, and before I was through the doors I heard the talk break out, and the godawful racket as derby hat and his young *amigo* started up again. Finn's place was back to business.

Trouble was, I knew Burrell was right; this little run-in of ours wasn't over. I might have walked out of Finn Mahoney's saloon with my hide, but I got the feeling I'd just walked into something else a whole lot worse.

Pretty soon, I'd know how bad it was likely to get.

3

Outside, there wasn't too much happening. Half a dozen or so of the more curious folks had ventured out of doors at the noise of the gunshot, but once they saw me step on to the walk with two pistols in hand they kept their distance. The gun Rufe Simmons had let fall was a .44 Remington Army. He'd let it rust more than was good for it, but it was a solid enough weapon all the same, if a mite heavy for my taste. Horse-trough was just down from the walk, by the hitching-rail. I pitched the gun in and let it sink, watching the bubbles burst and spread.

'That oughta do it,' I said. I reset the hammer on the Colt, and slipped it back into its pocket holster. Alice was a couple of yards in front as we went across the alley and on to the next block. Once we got into shade again she halted, and turned around.

'You saved my life back there, Miss Soledad,' Alice had found that melting smile of hers again. It went just fine with her pretty face and baby-blue eyes, I guess. 'But for you, those men might have killed me. I'm heartily grateful to you, believe me.'

'Let's you an' me talk business, Alice,' I said.

She caught the look on my face, and that smile slipped just a little.

'To be sure, your stake.' She fumbled inside the bandanna, struggling to get it open. 'You'll be wanting the money you gave to back me for the winning hand.'

'Not just that.' I shook my head. 'What I want is all the money I'm due to. An' that means every cent of mine that went into that game.'

She pulled up short at that, and now the smile was clear out of sight.

'Surely, you cannot be serious?' She frowned at me, trying to look puzzled. This time, though, it didn't work. 'You saw me win the game, Soledad. The money is mine.'

'What I saw you do was cheat at cards, Alice,' I said.

That caught her out, for sure. Her rosy pink face went white as a floursack, and I saw her hand clench up like it had ideas of its own. I dropped my own hand on to her wrist, and took a tight hold. It was the arm Simmons had grabbed, and I felt her flinch, struggling to break away.

'An' if you got a weapon hid, don't try for it,' I told her. 'I ain't in the mood. Right now I'm the best friend you're gonna find in Tylerville, Alice. Better do like I say.'

She thought about that for a while, scowling up into my face as she fought to make me let go. She could have saved herself the trouble. Maybe she had a strong grip, but I reckon I've had more practice, being a horse-breaker and all.

'My room is another block from here,' she said at last. 'If you come with me, we can settle the matter there in a civilized fashion. Now, if you would be so kind as to release me. Brawling on the street is rather undignified, don't you think?'

'Just so long as I get my money back,' I said.

I loosed my grip and she stood off, pouting and stroking her wrist like it was broken or something. Alice turned sharply and set off along the walk, and I strolled after her, keeping close behind. We made it to the next block, and up the splintery wooden steps to Rice's Hotel. Kind of a grand name for a dingy old flophouse that made Mahoney's place look like a palace, but there wasn't much else Tylerville had to offer in the hotel line. I'd been here before, and I knew.

Once inside we picked up the key and headed up the stairs to her room. The desk clerk gave me a strange kind of look as we went up by him. Seemed like he wasn't used to seeing two women head upstairs together, least of all when one of them's wearing men's clothes. Guess they lead a sheltered kind of life in Tylerville.

I waited in the darkened passage while Alice set the key into the lock, and opened up. The door creaked open and the pair of us stepped inside, me shoving it shut behind us and taking a good look around to make sure there was nobody else around to deal with.

'Just me, that's all,' Alice sounded like I'd offended her. She set down the bandanna on the bed, and sat beside it with a groan and twang of well-tried springs. 'Who else would I be keeping in my room, do you think?'

'That ain't for me to say, Alice,' I checked for someplace to sit. Didn't have to try too hard, there was but the one chair in the room. I turned it around and straddled, leaning my arms on the back to look over it at Alice on the bed. After years aboard horses, I find chairs are more comfortable that way. 'Now let's talk money, huh?'

'You said you saw me cheat back there.' She began to unfasten the bandanna, the heap of notes and coin spilling out on the bed. All the while she eyed me as though she didn't believe me. 'Is that all you're going to tell me?'

'Well, maybe not.' I slapped at a fly that came droning in overhead. Rice's place was just as strong on dust and flies as anywhere else in Tylerville, I figured. 'Fact is, I didn't see you do nothin', Alice. I just happen to know there's no way you could be holdin' four of a kind when Hildreth had two of them self-same kings in the deck.'

Her face went stony for a while, and she didn't answer, so I went ahead. 'You worked a holdout,' I told her. 'Worked it real good, too. Slickest thing I ever seen in my life — well, slick enough for me not to see a damn thing. They were all of 'em card-sharps, sure, but you're different class, Alice. You cheated a way better than they did, an' I reckon you earned their money. I just want what's mine.'

I quit at that, looking her straight in

the eye. After a minute or so the bleakness wore off her face and she nodded and shrugged.

'Very well, Soledad. I see you have me at a disadvantage.' She smiled, counting out the wad of tens and fives on the bed. Standing up, she came over and handed it to me. 'This is yours, I think.'

'*Gracias.*' I flipped through the bills and nodded approval. Alice had counted it up from memory without a hitch. Maybe she was the kind to keep track on every last cent, I thought. 'Looks like it's all here, right enough.'

I tucked it away in the billfold, and fitted it into the back pocket of my cords. It felt a way better there, I can tell you.

'I feel it's time for us to become a little better acquainted,' Alice said. She went across the room to where a bottle and glass rested in the shade by the window. 'Would you care for another drink, Soledad?'

'You wouldn't be tryin' to get me

drunk?' Seeing the sharper glint in her eyes, I grinned at her. 'Just funnin', Alice. Didn't mean nothin' by it.'

'If you say so.' She filled the glass and stood, bottle in one hand and glass in the other. 'We have only the one glass, I'm afraid.'

'So take it, an' hand me the bottle,' I said. I took it, and raised it to her as she raised the glass. '*Salud*, Alice.'

'Good health, Soledad.'

It was whiskey in the bottle, and whiskey is something I'm kind of familiar with when the chance comes along. This wasn't the best, but it was good enough. None of your turpentine and wood alcohol, that was for sure. I took a couple of swallows and set it down, savouring the taste. Seated back on the creaking bed, Alice smiled and sipped from her glass.

'I have the feeling you would like to know rather more about me. Is that right?'

'You could say that, Alice.' I studied the floating dust-specks in the room as I spoke. 'That your real name, Treharne?'

'It is.' Alice took a fresh sip at her glass. 'Or rather, it was my husband's, James Treharne. Both of us came over here from Cornwall eight years ago.'

'Cornwall, huh?' I thought about that, and it didn't mean a thing to me. 'That wouldn't be up in Canada someplace, would it?'

As soon as the words came out I knew it had been a dumb thing to say. The way she smiled at me above the rim of her glass was polite enough, but it made sure I knew just how dumb it was.

'Not Canada, Soledad,' Alice softly corrected. 'Cornwall's in England, the West Country they call it over there. James was a manager in a tin mine; he asked me to marry him and travel to the States. He had this idea we could make our fortunes.' She broke off then, and from the way her eyes clouded over you could tell she was thinking back to how it had been. 'Such a fine, handsome figure of a man he was,

Soledad! There was nothing I wouldn't have done for James, nothing at all.'

Yeah, reckon I've been there too, I thought. All the same, I didn't say it, just hoisted the bottle and took another pull at the whiskey. Tasted even better this time.

'So where's your husband now?' I wanted to know.

'I believe he's dead,' Alice said.

I looked up at her, and sure enough there were tears in her eyes. She was fighting to keep them back all right, but I could see it was a tough job for her. For a while it got kind of hard for me to say anything at all.

'Sure sorry to hear that, Alice,' I said.

'We had this saloon in St Louis.' She started talking in a rush, like she hadn't heard what I said. 'We weren't rich, but we made a living there. I think I could have stayed there and been happy, just the two of us together. But then he heard about the silver lode they'd struck in Walleye, not far from here. He was to wire me to join him once he'd registered a claim.'

She paused, struggling for breath, and pulled out a tiny handkerchief to dab at her eyes for a moment. When she looked up again, I nodded.

'Go ahead, Alice. I'm listenin',' I told her.

'I had word from him a week ago.' Alice sipped at her drink again before going on. 'He had staked a claim and was here in Tylerville to settle some other business; he didn't say what it was.' She took a breath, turning those tear-filled eyes on me again. 'He died here in Tylerville, Soledad. When I got here, the man at the stage station told me. Just two days before I arrived, he just fell down in the street and died. It was his heart, they said. Nothing they could do!'

Now it got too much for her, I guess, and she sobbed and shook to break a heart of stone. I was reaching out to comfort her but I didn't quite make it. At the time, I couldn't help but notice how in the midst of her grieving she

70

kept a tight hold on that whiskey glass, and didn't so much as spill a drop.

'That sure is hard to bear, Alice,' I allowed. It was about then that something else dawned on me, and set me to frowning on my own account. 'He died here a couple of days back, huh? How come none of them cardsharps said nothing? They must've heard you tell 'em your name was Treharne.'

'Yes, I thought it strange myself.' Alice snuffled a little, dabbing at the tearstains on her cheeks. 'After all, Mr Hildreth is undertaker here. He must have .. attended to James himself. I'm surprised he said nothing about it.'

'Yeah, that's what I thought,' I said. Which was true enough, but it wasn't all of it. What I didn't say, but what was going through my mind right then was that Hildreth and the others hadn't even looked surprised when she came out with her name. Like they might just have been expecting her all along. And what that meant, I

71

had no way of telling.

'He's buried here, in the cemetery,' Alice was saying. Her voice got through to me and I came out of the thinking spell, lifting the bottle again. Taking a swallow, I saw those blue eyes fixed on me like they were about to ask a favour. 'I intend to visit the grave tomorrow, before I travel on to Walleye and investigate his business affairs. If you could see your way to coming with me, I would surely welcome the company. I realize it would mean your staying here for a further night.'

'Well, now.' Tell truth, I was thinking I'd been in Tylerville long enough as it was, and had started to get itchy for the horse ranch back in Arizona. Then again, I reckoned I was getting to like Alice Treharne, and walking out on her didn't appear too neighbourly. 'Sure, Alice. I'll do it. Guess another night here ain't gonna make no difference.'

'Would you?' Alice had dried her tears. Now she sat up and smiled like the sun breaking out after a desert storm. 'That's truly kind of you, Soledad. I appreciate it, believe me.'

She took a fresh sip on the whiskey like she really appreciated that, too. Unless I missed my guess, the *dinero* she'd won had come in pretty handy for her. I had the feeling that the story about her last hundred dollars might not have been far from the truth. She'd needed to win more than Burrell and his pals, I figured.

I stayed quiet, and was looking for the bottle again when her voice reached for me. 'You were quite magnificent, back there,' Alice said at last. Above the rim of the glass, she watched me thoughtfully, like she wasn't too sure what she was seeing. 'I didn't realize you carried a pistol.'

'Didn't aim for you to see it,' I told her. 'Nor nobody else, neither. I'm here to sell horses, not to shoot no one. Not even dumb sons of bitches like Rufe Simmons.'

'You appear to know how to use it, from what I saw.'

'If I have to,' I shrugged, getting a mite tired of it all. 'Most times there ain't no need. How 'bout you, Alice? You a *pistolero* too, maybe?'

She chuckled at that, and her smile changed like she was about to share a secret. Alice slipped a hand inside the pocket of her gown, and came out with something she laid on the bed beside her winnings. I studied it a while, leaning over the back of the chair. It was a short-barrelled derringer, the kind they make over in England they tell me. So small, it could be hid and never noticed, but heavy enough to kill across a table.

'I'd say that was a .41, same as mine,' I offered.

'It shoots, that's all I know.' It was Alice's turn to shrug. She picked up the stingy gun and returned it to her pocket. 'I haven't had to fire it yet.'

'Let's hope that's how it stays,' I told her. 'Gunplay we kin do without, any time.' I set both hands to the chair back and pushed myself up, stepping clear

like I'd just got down from a horse. 'Nice talkin' to you, Alice, an' thanks for the money. Best be goin', I reckon.'

'Of course.' Alice stood up from the bed, her right hand stretched to shake. She had real nice manners, I have to admit. As we shook hands and let go, a startled look crossed her face and she glanced at me awkwardly. 'How very inconsiderate of me, Soledad. All this time up here, and I've done nothing but sit and talk of my own affairs. I don't know a single thing about you, beyond the fact that you're a horse-dealer and that you carry a pistol. You really must enlighten me, Soledad.'

'Some other time, OK.' I grinned, heading for the door. 'If I'm gonna stay the night here, better get myself a room. *Hasta la vista*, Alice.'

'Good evening, Soledad.' She smiled, one hand hoisted in farewell while the other kept a hold on the almost empty glass. 'See you in the morning.'

Sure hope so, I thought.

I ducked out through the door and

downstairs to the clerk at his desk. Seemed like there wasn't too much call for rooms this time of year, and I got myself a place to sleep without denting my billfold overmuch.

The room I'd booked was a couple of doors from Alice, but I guessed it might be better to stay clear for tonight. Once the door was shut I hauled off my hat and shirt, and checked under the bed for scorpions or rattlers. I found a little green-coloured lizard there, but I reckoned that wasn't so bad. Lizards I can live with, just about.

After the fun we'd had at Mahoney's it didn't take me long to sleep. Maybe I heard a scutter or so from the rats behind the wall, but that didn't signify. They weren't the two-legged kind. Anyhow, I needed all the shut-eye I could get.

I had a grave to visit, come the morning.

4

The cemetery was on a low hill outside town, and the grave we wanted was the furthest out. Just a hummock in the ground, the dirt more fresh-turned than the rest, but already drying out and cracking in the early morning heat. A few starved-looking blades of grass had begun to poke their way through in places. On top of the mound somebody had fixed two weathered lengths of wood and lashed them together in a makeshift cross. When you stood close, you could read the letters burned into the wood.

JIM TREHARNE
8.16.1888
R.I.P.

I tugged off my hat and stood back a way as Alice knelt down at her husband's grave. The handful of flowers she laid there had been plucked that morning, but the sun had already shrivelled them up, and they looked mighty pale and sickly on that heap of dirt. Tell truth, I reckoned if the two of us stayed up here much longer we were likely to get pretty shrivelled up ourselves. Not that I aimed to go telling her that right now.

'So this is what you've come to, Jim,' Alice told the mound of dirt where the flowers lay wilting. From the way she was talking I could tell she was near the end of her rope, and the grave had sense enough not to answer back. 'What a way to end, dying on the street in this godforsaken place. And it hasn't been easy on me, either. Why did you have to come here, Jim? Didn't I always tell you we should have stayed in St Louis?'

She broke down and sobbed, her slim shoulders heaving as the tears fell on that dry, sun-baked piece of dirt. That was when the other voice spoke up.

'I beg you, ma'am, don't distress

yourself,' the voice said. 'He is gone to a better place, be sure.'

I spun round real fast at the sound of that voice, feeling kind of foolish he'd got the drop on us so easy. He must have moved quieter than an Indian, I figured. Either that, or I'd been half asleep. Maybe a touch of both, to tell the truth. Turning, I saw a tall, wide-shouldered feller in a rusty black Prince Albert coat, standing there and nodding to us while he held a black, flat-crowned hat against his chest.

'Good morning to you, ladies.' His voice came out of his chest, too, strong and deep as a flash flood through an *arroyo*. I reckoned I felt it shake the ground under my feet as I listened. 'Reverend Reuben Hall, at your service.'

That big, powerful voice seemed out of line with the clothes he was wearing. The rusty coat was a size too small, pinching him at the shoulders, and the black pants rode ankle-high above heavy, workmen's boots. He'd lost a collar-stud and one side of his shirt-neck thrust out like a broken wing. The whole rig was white with alkali dust, and it looked like it had seen better days. Yet for all that, you wouldn't have dared to laugh at him. Under the threadbare clothes his frame was burly and strong as a stevedore's, the muscles bunching up against the tightness of the cloth. Eyeing him there, I was put in mind of a massive boulder in the middle of the desert, something that you wouldn't get to shift until it decided itself that it was time to go.

'With your permission, ma'am.' He stepped by me, nodding politely as he went on to where Alice knelt by the grave. The reverend halted just short of the mound, and bowed his head solemnly. 'Perhaps I might speak some word of comfort over the dear departed?'

His eyes fixed on Alice as he spoke, studying her like they didn't aim to miss a trick. He had a beaked eagle-ish kind of a face, the reverend, sober and dignified you might say, with a thick greying beard that hid the jaw from sight. His eyes were grey too, and with a straight, no-nonsense look to them. Watching Alice as she turned up her face to meet them, I could see she was taken by them.

'You're surely welcome, Reverend Hall,' Alice said. I don't rightly know what it was that woman had, but I swear that even with the tears making tracks down the dust that covered her face, she was just as pretty as always. And even at the graveside, I doubt the reverend was so dumb that he was likely to miss that fact.

'Most kind, ma'am,' says the holy man, and takes up position by the grave with his hat still clutched to his bosom. Alice and me both bent our heads as he prayed.

'Lord, show mercy to this poor pilgrim child,' the reverend boomed. His voice went thundering out across the plain towards the far mountains, and I saw a scared jack-rabbit spring out from a saltbush clump at the sudden noise, racing down the slope in fear of his life. The reverend seemed not to see him, rolling on like a river. 'Spare him from his sins, and bring him out of the valley to share a place at Thy table. Amen!'

'Amen,' I said after him. It seemed like the thing to do. And down on her knees by the grave, Alice said it too.

'Why, that was wonderful, Reverend.' She smiled now, dabbing at the tear-streaks as she got to her feet. 'What a comfort to us at such a time. Thank you so much!'

'Your servant, ma'am.' He shook her hand as she offered it to him, hint of a smile breaking through his grizzled beard. 'Do I take it that I have the pleasure of conversing with Mrs Alice Treharne?'

'Indeed you do, Reverend.' Alice beamed like a young girl at her first dance. Seemed it was an effort for her to let go his hand. 'The pleasure's mine, I do assure you.' She turned to where I stood apart from them, starting to feel like the fifth leg on a thoroughbred. 'This is my good friend Soledad. She has been a great help to me.'

'Delighted, Miss Soledad.' The reverend released her, leaned over to press my hand. I could be wrong, but I reckon he let go of me a whole lot quicker than he had my friend. Meeting those eyes as they cut clean through me, I cracked the best smile I had to hand.

'Same again, Reverend,' I told him.

'Couldn't help but notice you two ladies up here,' that booming voice was saying. 'It's my custom to visit these places of rest, after all. Besides, Mr Mahoney told me of your sad loss, and the least I could do was offer my condolences.' He paused, the grey eyes looking us over as he appeared to ponder something in his mind. 'He also informs me that you intend to travel to Walleye soon. That is where I'm headed.'

'How would Mr Mahoney know that,

I wonder?' For an instant Alice lost her smile, and her rosy little face took on a quarrelsome look. Catching the change in the weather, the reverend shrugged, all but splitting the seams of his rusty coat.

'From the folks at the stage station, I imagine.' The burly *hombre* glanced to the crossed laths of wood above the mound. 'I understand he fixed the cross here for your late husband. To be sure, he is a man with a good heart, though he plies an evil trade.'

'Sounds like his jaw must be healed some, the way you tell it,' I put in. I'd been feeling kind of guilty for a while now over the way we'd left Finn, sprawled out on the floor of his saloon, courtesy of Rufe Simmons. 'Reckon that has to be good news.'

'Merely bruised, he assures me.' The reverend's smile cracked through the grey of his beard. 'Quite an unpleasant scene in the saloon on that occasion, I gather?'

It was to Alice he looked this time,

and she wasn't slow to answer.

'Yes, most alarming.' The sour expression had gone, and she was back to belle of the ball again. 'Mr Mahoney was a regular gentleman, he did his best to defend me.'

'So I heard.' Reverend Hall nodded, his beaked face turning grim at the thought. 'Were the same thing to happen again, ma'am, I flatter myself I would do the same.'

'Mighty kind of you to say so, Reverend.' Alice smiled up at him with the words, those blue eyes all wide and little-girl-lost. You could see she was taken with him, and no mistake. The two of them were getting on so fine I felt like some kind of chaperon. Maybe that's why I said what I did.

'So you're headed for Walleye, Reverend,' I said. 'Way I heard it, that town don't have no time for preachers.'

Both of them turned to me as I spoke, and I guess something of the soreness must have shown in my voice, because Alice gave me a sharp kind of glance that would have slit a buffalo hide anyplace else. The reverend didn't appear too put out, though. He just looked down at me from the height he had, and smiled like he was humouring a salty kid.

'Nevertheless, I intend to go there,' the reverend told me. 'Walleye is a Godless place, that much is plain. But I am called for a purpose, and when the Lord commands He will not be gainsaid. Walleye shall see the light, and resign its sinful ways.' He paused, and shrugged those broad shoulders again, at considerable risk to his tailoring. 'Besides, Miss Soledad, before I heard the call I worked as a blacksmith, and I still practise the trade when required. There is no town I know of that has no use for a blacksmith, and it is a calling not to be despised. After all, our Saviour worked with His hands. He was a carpenter, was He not?'

'Yeah, reckon you got me there, Reverend,' I said.

After what I'd seen in the last day or

so, I figured Reverend Hall could do worse than start his good work right here in Tylerville. The place sure seemed like it could use a little Christian charity. Then again, I guessed that was his business, not mine.

'It seems we are to embark on the same journey, Mrs Treharne,' the reverend was back to Alice again, voice questioning as he clutched his hat with both bony hands. 'If you are agreeable, I can offer you a seat beside me on my wagon. It is a poor thing, that carries the tools of my trade, but the two of us could travel in company.' His beaked face cracked to a smile again. 'It would certainly be a pleasure for me.'

'Most kind of you, Reverend. I'd be delighted.' Alice shone back at him like sunlight, ducking her blonde head in its prim little bonnet. Glancing towards me, she halted, unsure for a moment. 'Of course, Soledad must come too. I won't hear of our leaving her behind. You will come with us as far as Walleye, won't you, Soledad?'

I met those eyes with their pleading look, and sighed, knowing when I was beaten. Fact is, travelling to Walleye was the last thing I'd had in mind. Once we got back from the graveyard I was planning to fit myself around a good breakfast, see to my horse and head back for the horse ranch in Arizona. But once Alice looked at you that way, it was hard to tell her no. Wasn't just me had a problem with her, I reckon it went for just about anybody she met, Burrell and his pals excepted. And when I thought it over, Walleye wasn't so far out of my way that I couldn't tag along.

'If that's the way you want it, Alice,' I told her.

'Why, of course I do!' She laughed, and laid her hand on my arm like she was out to reassure me. 'After all the help you've given me, I'd surely welcome you, Soledad. And I'm sure the reverend here won't mind.'

Seeing the look on the face of the

'That's a lady you're talking about, mister,' the reverend said. He looked that hulking grizzly right in the eye as he said it. 'I'll thank you to keep a civil tongue in your head for the future. Now, if you'll excuse us.'

He clapped the battered old hat on his head, Alice letting go his arm, and set both hands against Simmons' chest, easing him back and out of the way. The thick-set *hombre* snarled and dug his heels, trying to hold his ground, but it seemed like the reverend could more than match him. Simmons went backwards, swearing and gritting his teeth. A couple of paces back he staggered and stayed put as the reverend walked Alice right on by him for the town.

'Easy on the language too, if you don't mind,' the preacher told him.

I was catching the others up, and the three of us were almost back into Tylerville, when I heard Vaughan Burrell call out behind me.

'Remember, you ain't in Walleye yet!' he ruddy-faced *hombre* shouted. I

reverend, I figured she needn't have asked.

'Not at all, ma'am.' He managed a smile of his own, but I reckoned he found it more of an effort this time around. 'Miss Soledad is most welcome to accompany us.'

'Two of you can share the wagon, Reverend,' I told him. 'I'll be ridin', like always.'

'To be sure,' he nodded, his eyes with Alice again. 'Well, it's been a real pleasure meeting you ladies, even under these mournful circumstances. If you're ready to leave, we can return to the town now.'

He smiled, offering his arm to Alice, and she hung on to it, beaming fit to bust. The three of us left the graveyard and headed back down the slope towards Tylerville. By now the sun was fully risen, and the heat was fierce enough to make you catch your breath. I'd worked up quite a sweat on my own account by the time we reached the edge of town. Long before we got to the foot of the slope, I could see the three *hombres* who stood there waiting for us to arrive.

'Morning ladies, Reverend,' Vaughan Burrell touched the brim of his neat Stetson hat. This time he didn't trouble to smile, eyes cold in that ruddy, fresh-coloured face of his as he rested both thumbs in his hand-tooled leather belt. 'Visiting the dear departed, I see.'

Behind him, Rufe Simmons and that little weasel Hildreth said nothing, their eyes mean and hard as they looked us over. I saw Alice take a breath and bite on her lip, and the reverend's hands clench up tight on the hat he was holding, and got ready for more unpleasantness to come.

'Hear tell you're headed for Walleye, Mrs Treharne?' Burrell enquired, and Alice nodded, her own glance decidedly chilly as it rested on him.

'That's so, Mr Burrell.' Alice indicated the tall *hombre* in the dust-covered black coat whose arm she gripped. 'The Reverend Hall here has kindly offered to take me there.'

Burrell took that in, not answering for a while. Against the threadbare clothes the preacher wore, his fancy range gear looked sharper than ever, catching the sun with its polished clasps and silver conchos. Now Burrell shifted his glance and studied the tall, bearded *hombre* who towered above him.

'Is that so?' Burrell murmured. It wasn't a friendly enquiry.

'Better watch out for her, Reverend,' Rufe Simmons leered, yellow teeth breaking the black mass of stubble. 'She cheats at cards, is what I heard.'

I saw Hildreth and Burrell grin alon[g] with him, and, but for the reverer[d] being there, I might have been tempt[ed] to punch that ugly sonofabitch right [in] the nose, even if he killed me after. A[s] turned out, I needn't have worried. [The] reverend took a step closer so tha[t he] and Simmons faced each other. S[eeing] them close to, I realized that [the] preacher was tall enough to look [down] on Simmons as well.

90   91

caught the menace in his voice, sensing the cold eyes fixed on my back. 'An' if you do get there, you're gonna wish you never made it!'

I didn't stop, walking on to join Alice and the reverend. All the same, what I'd just heard gave me a bad feeling. Like Burrell knew something we didn't, and none of it good.

That feeling stayed with me all the way back into Tylerville.

5

We were camped halfway to Walleye, and barely through eating our beans and sourdough bread, when we saw the first of the dust heading our way. My roan horse had his ears pricked and was shifting around kind of nervous, so I crossed over and talked to him a while, stroking him down till he was quiet. That's where I was when the line of horsemen came over the crest and walked their mounts down to meet us, the riders at either end of the line fanning out wide to keep us covered from both sides. So far not a man had drawn his gun. Maybe they figured they didn't need to.

'No call for you to use that pistol, lady!' the first horseman called to me. He reined in, leaning forward on the saddlehorn, and touched his hatbrim to the folks behind me. 'Afternoon,

Reverend, Mrs Treharne.'

He was an oldster, somewhere the wrong side of sixty at a guess, with a massive gut that overhung his gunbelt like a pot-bellied stove. His face was dark from the sun, gullied with wrinkles, and half of it was hidden behind a white longhorn moustache stained brown with tobacco juice around the mouth. Right now he didn't worry me as much as the *hombres* he had with him. I saw Brocklehurst and Ashman, and Rufe Simmons there behind him. Worse, I saw Vaughan Burrell sitting alongside the oldster and smiling like he'd struck gold. I knew then it had to be as bad as it could get.

'Zeb Mulgrew,' the old man said. He thumbed the tin star pinned to his vest. 'I'm county sheriff, an' here on business. These fellers with me are a legally raised posse.'

'Perhaps you'll be good enough to explain the reason for this intrusion,' the reverend said, in the stiffest voice I'd heard from him so far.

'No need to worry, Reverend,' Mulgrew told him. 'Our business is with Miss Soledad here, an' it won't wait.'

'So let's hear it,' I said.

'You sold six horses to Mr Burrell in Tylerville yesterday. That right?'

'Sure I did.' I looked to where Burrell sat smirking all over his face. 'Why not ask him, Sheriff? He oughta have the bill of sale I gave him.'

Now Mulgrew didn't smile one bit, that gullied face mighty serious back of the white moustache.

'Gonna have to take you in, Miss Soledad,' the oldster said. He laid a hand on the .45 Army in his belt that same moment. 'Them six horses was stolen, an' I got me witnesses to prove it.'

Now I figured I'd heard it all. It was some while before I rounded up my breath to answer him.

'The hell you say!' Mulgrew had me so mad, I reckoned I was about to choke. 'What kind of witnesses?'

'Maybe you'd better tell her, Jake,' Burrell said. That cold edge was back in his voice.

'Them's our horses, Sheriff!' Jake Brocklehurst edged forward, calling out. Under that wide-brimmed hat he wore, his pinched little face was eager and flushed, like he couldn't wait to get out his lines. 'Me an' Kirk here set up our own ranch a couple of months back, over by Spanish Creek. Lost these critters but a week ago, we been lookin' ever since!'

I saw the sly, sideways glance he gave to Burrell as he talked, and the buck-toothed grin that split Kirk Ashman's horsey face, and just about boiled over.

'Why, you lyin' sons of bitches!' I said.

You could tell they didn't care for that. Brocklehurst, Ashman and Simmons all had their hands on their pistol-butts quicker than you could whittle a stick, and some of the other folks in the posse started to act mighty tense. I reminded myself that I wasn't Bill Hickock, and laid the .41 pistol down on the ground, stepping backward.

'That's a whole lot better, Miss Soledad,' Sheriff Mulgrew said. The oldster shifted half around in his saddle, looking once more to Brocklehurst and Ashman. 'Heard about you boys takin' up ranchin', Jake, but I didn't hear nothin' 'bout raisin' horses. You sure you got that right, now?'

'Sure we are, Sheriff.' Brocklehurst had started to look a mite uncomfortable. His eyes went sideways to Burrell again, as if he wanted help. 'Ain't that so, Mr Burrell?'

'He's telling the truth, Sheriff,' Burrell said. All the time that greasy smile stayed on his lips. I figured it was a wonder the lightning didn't strike him as he spoke.

'If you say so, Mr Burrell.' Mulgrew didn't sound altogether convinced by what he heard. All the same he turned back to me, his moustached-leather face sombre as a hanging judge. 'Looks like you're comin' back with us to Tylerville, lady.' He broke off, his glance easing over to where the reverend and Alice stood side by side, both looking like they were still coming out of some kind of daze. 'Reverend, we got no call to detain you. Reckon you an' Mrs Treharne can go on to Walleye if you've a mind.'

I saw that smile vanish from Burrell's face in an instant, and he and his pals began to look out-smarted. Rufe Simmons, though, burst forward to speak.

'Hold on, Sheriff!' The grizzly wasn't smiling either, though with him it didn't make too much difference. Simmons flicked his halter-rope to indicate the standing pair by the wagon, his voice angry and thick. 'These two are in it with her, dammit! Why in hell ain't you gonna arrest 'em all?'

'He's right, Sheriff.' Vaughan Burrell struggled to get back his smile, his cold eyes on the lawman. 'The two women are working together, no doubt of it, and the preacher could well be an accomplice. And don't forget, Mrs Treharne here cheated us of a substantial sum in a card game yesterday.'

'Yeah, Mr Burrell. Reckon I heard about your card games.' Mulgrew wasn't impressed, and his hard voice showed it. The oldster gave Burrell a scornful look, and puckered up to spit in the dust by his horse's feet. 'Best we don't look into that too close, seems to me. Right now there ain't no way of tyin' these two in with the horse deal, an' you know it. You want 'em arrested, better think of somethin' else.'

Burrell stayed quiet after that, but from the way he sat there fuming you could tell he was thinking plenty, and none of it good. Same went for Simmons and the others. The three of them looked like they'd just been fed a peck of cascara. Mulgrew was getting down from his horse, and I was all set to go with them, when Alice found her voice.

'Just a moment, Sheriff!' She called out so sharply it froze them in their tracks, the whole posse dumbstruck as they turned and listened. Alice faced them all, that china-doll figure drawn stiff and straight and her head held high. 'Do you gentlemen think you're going to send me on to Walleye without so much as a by your leave, while you take my friend back and hang her for a crime she never committed?' She fixed on the sheriff, those blue eyes blazing fire. 'I shall return with you to Tylerville, Mr Mulgrew, and you may be sure I intend to see justice done.'

It was one of the bravest things I ever saw. That slender little woman standing there with only the preacher by her, not a trace of fear in her pretty young face as she took on that whole bunch of horsemen and their guns. This wasn't the toughest hole I've ever found myself in. Believe it or not, I've met fellers a way harder than Burrell or Simmons could imagine in their worst dreams, but I doubt if Alice ever had. She could have gone on to Walleye and left me to them, but she didn't, and that's something I won't forget. Seeing her talk them down that way, I knew for sure there was more to Alice than cheating at cards. I'd done right when I chose her for a friend, back at Finn Mahoney's.

'Well now.' Mulgrew sounded as thrown as everybody else. The oldster raised bushy eye-brows, studying Alice as if he'd just seen her plain. 'If that's the way you feel about it, ma'am, ain't nothin' to stop you comin' back.'

'You may be sure there is not, Sheriff.' Alice smiled at him, tight-lipped.

'And I shall come with you, dear lady.' Now the reverend got into the act, grim-faced as he laid a protecting hand on her shoulder. 'It would scarcely be Christian to abandon you or your friend at such a time.' He glared at the lawman as if he'd just been insulted himself. 'I shall accompany you to Tylerville, never fear.'

'I told you they was in it together!' Rufe Simmons shouted. Beside him Vaughan Burrell nodded agreement, his fresh-coloured features cold and unsmiling. At the look I sent them, both men stayed quiet.

'You got your wish, Burrell,' I told him. 'We're comin' back to Tylerville, like you wanted. Only don't put money on watchin' me hang just yet; I aim to live a while.'

He didn't answer, but those cold eyes told me everything. Burrell had the deck ready and stacked, and for all I knew the jury was already in his pocket. For the first time it got through to me that I might not walk out of this business alive. It wasn't a feeling I'd wish on anyone, better believe it.

'Looks like I'm your prisoner,' I said to Mulgrew. Glancing back to the others, I forced a smile. 'Thanks, Alice. You too, Reverend.'

They said nothing, looking stunned, and I stayed by the roan as Mulgrew and his posse climbed down from their saddles. Pretty soon, I knew, we'd be riding again.

* ★ *

Sound of howling roused me, and I came awake, shivering in the cold. We were camped in the badlands halfway back to Tylerville, and the night was chill and blacker than a shroud. A bunch of coyotes were calling one to another 'way off into the hills, and their howls drifted across to where I was lying. It had been enough to wake me a few seconds back.

I sat up, hugging the saddle blanket around me to keep out the chill, and looked around. Mulgrew and his posse were bedded down and sleeping, if their snores were anything to go by. Same went for Alice and the reverend, though I didn't hear Alice snore. Reverend had let her sleep in the wagon while he rolled himself in a tarp by the nearside wheels. They'd set me apart from the rest, close to the edge of the camp.

Burrell hadn't liked it, but Mulgrew figured I wouldn't try to run. The feller who had the job of sentry was sitting right alongside me, anyhow. His name was Coleman, and he ran the dry goods store in Tylerville. Right this minute he was hunched over his old Sharps carbine with his eyes half-shut, doing his best to stay awake.

Just as well we weren't in Apache country, I thought.

I was still pondering this and feeling kind of thankful when I heard a shuffling noise, and saw one of the *hombres* beyond me throw off his blankets and get up, heading towards us. That jarred Coleman out of his slumbers, and the storekeeper swung round with the carbine lifting as he moved.

'Take it easy, Ben,' Vaughan Burrell said. 'Reckon it's my watch, ain't it?'

Coleman frowned, staring at him as if he wasn't too sure, and Burrell sighed. He leaned forward, and brought a rolled bunch of five and ten-dollar notes from his pocket, pressing them into the storeman's hand. Coleman still eyed him unsurely for a while, but not so much as before, and I saw him stow the dollars away into his coat.

'Go take a walk, Ben,' Burrell told him. 'I got business with the lady here.'

Coleman gulped like he was swallowing something too big for his gullet, and laid the carbine down. Burrell stayed watching as the storekeeper paced away around the far side of camp. Once he was out of sight, he turned to me.

'Just you and me, Soledad,' Burrell was smiling again. In the darkness I saw his eyes gleam, hard and cold. 'Nobody else to hear us. Time for you to be a little co-operative, wouldn't you say?'

'So what you got in mind, Burrell?' I asked. By now I had a pretty good idea.

'I think you know.' He was on his knees beside me, and moving closer. Pity the carbine was out of my reach, I thought. 'Play along with me this time, I might just be persuaded to overlook the horse-thieving business. We all make mistakes, after all.'

'You just did, Burrell,' I told him.

'I think not.' His face was close to me now, his breath warm in my face as that tight smile all but touched me. 'You've caused me a peck of trouble, lady. Time I had me some payment.'

His hand came hard over my mouth as I started to cry out, his weight pushing me backwards to the ground. I twisted and broke out from under him, rolling halfway clear, and jabbed up with my knee as he lunged in again. He leaned sideways from it, grunting as my knee thudded against the inside of his thigh. It froze him for an instant and I scrambled away from him, diving for the carbine that Coleman had left behind. Burrell caught a hold of my ankle and heaved and I went down hard, the breath slamming out of me as I hit the dirt belly-down. He tried to hang on to me and I kicked out backwards, my heel catching him somewhere in the face. Burrell yelled out and let go his grip, and I rolled again, struggling to get up. I was halfway back to my feet as Vaughan Burrell charged in for me again, and by now my blood was up all right. He came at me wide open and I swung my boot where I'd aimed it first, kicking like a mule. This time I got him clean. Vaughan Burrell folded and went down, the breath coming out of him like a locomotive whistle as he clasped both hands to his prize collection. He stayed down, rocking against the dirt as he gasped and moaned.

My temper was still running pretty hot, and I was set to kick him again when more noise broke out behind me, and what felt like a carpenter's vice caught hold of me round the shoulders, pinning my arms to my sides and dragging me away from the man on the ground.

'Salty bitch, ain't you?' Rufe Simmons muttered. I caught a gust of his breath, and fought to turn my head away. 'Oughta bust your neck right now, goddammit!'

He crushed me tighter to him, hoisting me off the ground and threatening to stave my ribs. I was about to stop breathing altogether when I heard Mulgrew call out.

'All right, Simmons! That's enough!' The sheriff barrelled up against the dark, pistol drawn and leathery face furious behind the longhorn moustache. 'Put her down, you hear?'

'She was tryin' to escape, Sheriff,' Simmons offered. He saw the gun in the lawman's hand and loosened his grip. I stumbled clear, wheezing and fighting for breath. 'We was just stoppin' her, is all.'

'Is that right?' Mulgrew didn't look at Rufe Simmons, his eyes on me as Burrell still moaned on the ground nearby. I shook my head.

'No, it ain't,' I told him. 'Ain't moved from here all night.'

'So what was it?' the oldster demanded, and I nodded towards Burrell.

'Reckon you can work it out, Sheriff,' I said.

'That bitch just tried to cripple me, damn it!' Burrell gasped, his ruddy face puckering up as he clutched both hands to his mistreated valuables. He glared up at Mulgrew, sweat standing out on his forehead. 'What do you aim to do about it?'

'Not a thing,' the sheriff told him. Mulgrew eyed the man at his feet disgustedly, his voice cracking harsh as a whip. 'You stay clear of her from now on, Burrell. You hear me good?'

Burrell gasped and flinched like he'd been hit again, and for a while he could barely speak at all for rage.

'You know who you're talking to, Sheriff?' Burrell's voice was mean, unforgiving. 'Tylerville is my town, Mulgrew. Ain't a stick or a stone back there don't have my brand on it. Best you should remember that, maybe?'

'I answer to the county,' the sheriff told him. 'That's bigger than you an' me both, Burrell. Now act civilized, or you'll go back to Tylerville in irons. An' if you try this again, I'll shoot you like a dog; you got that?'

Burrell got up with an effort, still clutching at himself as he rose.

'I don't aim to forget this, Sheriff.' He bit the words through his teeth.

'Just be sure you don't, Mr Burrell.' Mulgrew shoved the pistol into his belt. The lawman turned, yelling out to the oncoming possemen. 'Where the hell is Coleman? He was supposed to be sentry here!'

He stormed off, aiming to find the storekeeper in the crowd. If I'd had the time, I might even have felt a little sorry for Coleman. As it was, I kept my eyes on Vaughan Burrell as he staggered awkwardly by me, holding on to Rufe Simmons as he went.

'Don't worry, bitch,' Burrell told me. 'I'll see you hang, and soon.'

I didn't say anything, watching the two of them stumble away and back to their blankets. Right now I didn't seem to see Alice and the reverend as they came in towards me, my mind in another place. All at once the night was a way colder than before, and the wind blew clean through my bones.

I figured I could already feel that rope around my neck.

6

'You reckon you kin prove them horses are yours?' Mulgrew asked.

He pushed back the old bentwood chair until its front legs left the ground, and rocked unsteadily on the two that still rested against the floor. The jailhouse had its blinds drawn against the sunlight, but it got through all the same, tawny blades of light spilling across the hard dirt floor and picking out the spur-scarred desk and the tattered posters on the walls. From where I leaned up against the bars of the cell, I studied those old faded pictures. Rewards for outlaws, fellers who killed and robbed stages, or ran off cattle across the border. Could be there were a few horse-thieves among them, I thought.

'They all had my brand on 'em when I saw 'em last,' I said. 'Sloped S, that's for Soledad in case you ain't noticed. Did you get to take a look at 'em, then?'

'Sure did.' Mulgrew balanced on those spindly chair legs so long I was all but sweating in case he went over backwards. Just in time he brought all four legs down to earth again, frowning as he looked my way. 'Lady, I got to tell you they ain't wearin' a Sloped S no more. What they got now is a real big dollar sign, an' that's Jake an' Kirk's brand. Bar 8, they call it.'

'The bastards!' I'd been expecting something like this, but it didn't make it any easier to take. 'They must've used runnin' irons, damn it!'

'Maybe, an' maybe not.' The sheriff peered closer, squinting his eyes against the fierce light inside the room. 'Fact is, it's the brand they claim, an' right now it don't look like you got too much goin' for you, Miss Soledad. An' easy on the language, too, if you don't mind.'

'Yeah, guess you're right.' I simmered down a little, leaning more easily on the steel bars of the cell. It had been one hell of a time they'd given me since I first landed in Tylerville, and I figured it was beginning to wear the starch out of me by now. 'Thanks for pullin' me out from under Rufe Simmons, anyhow. Dumb son might just have hugged me to death.'

'Don't mention it.' Mulgrew reached into his vest for a thick tobacco plug, bit off the end and chewed contentedly. 'Tell you the truth, lady, I'd as soon make friends with a diamondback rattler as Vaughan Burrell, but I got to admit he's worked this one out. He has him some witnesses, an' now he's got evidence. You don't have a thing.'

'So now you're gonna sit by an' see me hang, huh?'

'Not me, Miss Soledad.' Mulgrew reared his chair back and spat a brownish stream into the brass cuspidor on the floor beside him. 'That's Judge Garrison's job, I reckon. He'll be over here Wednesday to try your case, an' we'll go along with what he has to say.

If it comes to a hangin', ain't no sheriff born is gonna tell him no.'

'Damn it, Mulgrew! You know I'm innocent.'

'Don't know nothin' of the kind, Miss Soledad.' Mulgrew bit a fresh hunk from the plug, leathery features thoughtful as he chewed. 'Seems to me you told it straight up to now, but that's just a feelin', an' it's only me that has it. You got to prove it, lady.'

'Yeah, to a Tylerville jury,' I said.

Mulgrew stopped chewing for a full second at that. When he spoke again, it was like I'd upset him real bad.

'Now that I don't care to hear,' the sheriff said. 'There's good folks here like everywhere, an' they ain't all in Burrell's pocket.' He fell quiet, chewing his wad and jetting the liquid into the spittoon, before going on. 'All I done is tell you the way things are, an' what I seen. Was I you, I'd save my breath for Wednesday. Believe me, you're gonna need it.'

'Whatever you say,' I told him.

I stepped back from the cell door, heading for my bunk. I made the journey a mite unsteadily, on account of I was wearing only the one boot. Alice had taken the other one to have stitches put into the leather, and she was due to meet up with the reverend after. They'd both been in to pay their respects while I was in the jailhouse. Finn Mahoney had been over, too, cracking jokes about the bruised lump Simmons had left on his jaw, and trying to keep my spirits up. Mulgrew was right; they weren't all bad in Tylerville. Trouble was, there were enough crooked ones to see me on to the end of that rope. I sure appreciated my three friends visiting, but I couldn't help feeling they were most likely wasting their time.

Mulgrew was just about at the end of his tobacco plug, and I was glad that I couldn't see the inside of the spittoon, when one of the deputies arrived to take over. He wasn't no more than a kid, seventeen or eighteen at a guess, with a long spindle-legged frame that seemed all knees and elbows, as if they'd poured him into the wrong-size body and he couldn't get out. He slid into the chair as Mulgrew left it, crossing both hands over his narrow middle like a gentleman of leisure.

'Your watch, kid,' the sheriff told him. 'An' no sleepin' on the job, remember?'

'Sure thing, Sheriff,' the youngster grinned. Mulgrew was already out of the door by the time he'd finished the sentence. Heading for Finn Mahoney's, I was willing to bet. The kid let him go, swinging long legs up on to the desk as he rubbed a shine into the tin star on his vest. All the time his eyes stayed with me.

'You're Miss Soledad, ain't you?' he offered, and I gave him a nod. 'Name's Kennedy, ma'am, Boone Kennedy, deputy to Sheriff Mulgrew. Mighty pleased to make your acquaintance.'

'Likewise, Mr Kennedy.' Looking him over, it was hard not to smile. His unshaved face was still smooth as a boy's, with the snub nose and spatter of freckles that would have been fine on a ten year old. This must be what they meant by giving a boy a man's job, I thought. 'Pity the circumstances ain't a little better, is all.'

'Yeah, ma'am. That's right enough.' He laughed at that, his kid's face wrinkling up as the grin cut it wide. When he sobered down again, his eyes gave me kind of a curious stare. 'Sheriff tells me you're pretty well known, Miss Soledad. You the lady shot Phil Gruber dead, ain't you?'

'That's right,' I told him. Guess I might have sounded a little tired. It was something I'd had to say to plenty of folks in my time.

'Wow.' Boone Kennedy's mouth was open, and he stared at me like he hadn't seen me before. 'How about that! Hear tell he was quite some gun-slinger, Miss Soledad.'

'He was a killer, an' fast with a gun. I was just smart enough not to be in front of him when I shot.' Now I was tired all right, and it showed in my voice. 'Nothing fine 'bout killin' folks, son. Somethin' you do when you have to, that's all. Now raisin' a horse herd, that takes talent an' you'd better believe it.'

'Guess you're right, ma'am.' The kid ducked his head, but I knew he wasn't listening. He figured wearing a star and shooting off a gun was hero stuff, just like they all did. 'All the same, sure must have been somethin' to see.'

I didn't answer, shutting my eyes as I leaned my head to the bars. I could have told the kid there was nothing to it, that I'd killed Gruber from behind with a .22 pocket pistol when he'd outdrawn a friend of mine, but I didn't try. He wouldn't listen, because it wasn't the kind of answer he wanted to hear. So I stayed quiet, and let him draw the picture the way he liked it.

Boone Kennedy had dropped into silence himself and was busy flicking his hat at a hovering fly when the door of the jailhouse opened and Alice Treharne stepped inside.

'Why, good evening, Deputy.' Alice smiled to light up the room. She was just as damn pretty as when I saw her first, knocking him dead with those big blue eyes of hers. 'I wasn't expecting to find you here. I declare, you quite startled me!'

Boone Kennedy had swung his long legs off the desk and catapulted out of that chair faster than a ricochet off a rock. He was standing there grinning and dusting his levis with his hat by the time she got through the door. From the look on his face, you could tell he figured Christmas had come early.

'Sure is a pleasure, ma'am.' The kid's face flushed up hotter than a furnace as he spoke. 'Anythin' I kin do for you?'

Alice didn't answer right away, her head tipped back as she beamed up at him. I saw she was holding my boot in both hands.

'My, Deputy, you're taller than I thought.' Alice was about as close as was decent in the circumstances, her blue eyes wider than ever. 'Better not grow too much further, we'll need to have the ceiling raised.'

'Name's Boone Kennedy, ma'am. Glad to meet you.' The youngster shoved out a bony hand towards her. Any minute now, I figured, his face would burst into flames.

'Happy to meet you too, Boone.' Alice smiled and shook hands, keeping her hold on the boot. 'Alice Treharne, I think you know that already. I've just brought back my friend's boot from the cobbler's. All right if I hand it over?'

'Maybe I better do that, ma'am. Sheriff Mulgrew told me no sleepin' on the job.' The deputy eyed the newly stitched boot warily, like it was about to bite him. 'Mind if I take a look first?'

'Not at all.' Alice gave that soft little chuckle of hers, shaking her bonneted head. 'No guns or knives in there, I do assure you. Please, be my guest.'

She waited until he peered carefully inside the boot, and shot a swift glance in my direction. Alice winked an eye, and turned back. That was all, but I needed no more. That wink told me that something was happening here, and it was no accident that Alice had come in here so soon after Mulgrew had gone. Now she smiled on, studying the tattered posters on the walls, the chained pistols and the shotguns on their racks as Kennedy handed the boot in through the bars.

'Thanks, Alice.' I eyed the fresh stitching and nodded. Feller had done a good job, from what I could see. 'Sure do appreciate it.'

Alice, though, seemed not to hear, scanning the room like she'd never seen it before.

'What a fascinating place you have here, Deputy.' She stepped across the room, peering more closely at the posters on the wall. 'And what are these for, do you suppose?'

'Wanted posters, ma'am,' Boone Kennedy grinned, edging over to join her. He stood as close up as he dared, pointing them out to her like a teacher to a girl still in school. 'These are for the badmen we ain't caught yet; mostly they're offerin' a reward dead or alive. See here' — he took hold of her arm, indicating one of the tattered pictures — 'that's Jim Eagles, the train-robber. They got three thousand dollars on him.'

'Imagine that!' Alice shook her head, smiling as she eased out of his grip. She moved back to the desk, touching the set of steel cuffs that lay there. 'And this is for holding violent prisoners, I presume?'

'Right again, ma'am.' Kennedy started towards her, still sporting that dumb grin. He halted as she glanced by him to the shotgun that was chained to its rack on the wall behind.

'I see you are well stocked for weapons.' Alice sounded most impressed. 'No chance of escape from here, I think.'

'That's right, ma'am.' Kennedy nodded amiably. 'Not a chance.'

'Some of them are a little high on the wall. That shotgun, for instance.' Alice eyed the shackled weapon, seeming to frown in thought. 'That looks a little too high to reach from here, even for someone as tall as yourself.'

I was already busy hauling on my boot, watching all the while. I figured I knew the way things were going.

'Oh no, ma'am.' Kennedy turned from her eagerly, stretching upward. 'I can reach it from here just fine.'

'You'll oblige me by standing quite still, Deputy,' Alice said.

She wasn't smiling any more, and her voice had changed in a moment. All at once it had a tight, waspish sound to it. Like a schoolmarm, only meaner. Kennedy froze at the sound of it, turning his head. He found himself looking down the short twin barrels of the derringer pistol she'd just drawn out of her bosom, and now levelled on him.

'Turn around, and keep both your hands raised.' She saw him hesitate for an instant, and her voice sharpened up a notch. 'Mr Kennedy, I was trained in the use of firearms by Lieutenant Caleb Whittaker of the 95th Regiment, and he counted me an excellent shot. I have no wish to kill a man, but if you cross me further I shall shoot you dead. Am I understood?'

Boone Kennedy tried to speak, and couldn't. From the stunned look he gave her I could see he still didn't believe it. He gasped, nodding his head.

'Take the key, and unlock the door to that cell,' Alice told him. 'And no noise, or I shall be forced to shoot.'

'Yes, ma'am.' It sounded like a whimper. The kid stumbled over to the bunch of keys on the desk, and on to the cell door. Once that key had turned in the lock, I was out of there faster than a shot.

'Now, inside, and put out your hands through the bars.'

Kennedy lurched past me like a man in a dream, and I shut the door on him. I was way ahead of the game now. I had the door locked as soon as he got inside, pitched the keys away far side of the room, and took the cuffs from Alice, who still held the stingy gun to his head. I snapped the cuffs shut on his wrists as those bony hands came through the bars, and Boone Kennedy was well and truly hog-tied.

'This ain't hardly right, Miss Soledad.' The kid had trouble getting out the words, like something was choking him. He looked at me pleading with his eyes, and I felt kind of sorry for him. He was just a kid, after all. He'd taken a licking, and now he looked ready to cry.

'Nothin' personal, son,' I told him. 'I'm just a mite averse to bein' hung, is all.'

He didn't answer, fighting to keep his lip from trembling. Alice kept the gun on him as she pushed me towards the back door of the jailhouse.

'If I hear you call out, I shall come back,' she told the handcuffed deputy. 'And believe me, I shall not miss.'

Boone Kennedy said nothing, biting

his lip as he fought the cuffs. I hauled the back door open and dived outside, Alice following at a run.

We came out on to a straggle of shacks and waste ground not far from the corrals, thick with spiny brush and trash from the buildings on Front Street. We'd barely got outside when a low, whooshing roar broke the quiet, and flames shot up fierce and high against the dusk. It was from someplace on Front Street, I couldn't be sure where, but it was some fire all right. Bright orange and yellow streamers of flame went roaring skywards, and after them a rolling black blanket of smoke. You could see the bright sparks showering in the air, and hear the fire booming underneath as wood from the building crackled and gave way to it. I hadn't seen anything like it since I hit Laredo on the Fourth of July a couple of years back. Any other time, I might have stayed to watch.

'Over here, Miss Soledad! Hurry!' That was the reverend's voice. I saw him then, tall and upright as a gatepost in the shadow of the jailhouse wall, holding the ropes on three fretting horses. I didn't need urging, and I was up and aboard the bay that was nearest as Alice ran for a mount of her own. All three of us were in the saddle and ready to ride as voices yelled from the street beyond. From the sound of it, though, they were heading for the fire, not coming after us. A few seconds later another figure stumbled into sight around the corner of the block.

'That oughta hold 'em!' Finn Mahoney said. He was out of breath like he'd been running hard, and his face and hands were smeared with what I figured must be coal-oil, but his broad brown features were grinning like I'd never seen before. Catching sight of us he nodded, his curled red hair reflected in the light of the flames. 'That's Luke Hildreth's place yonder. He had it comin', the cheatin' little bastard!' Seeing Alice's expression, and the frown of the reverend, he ducked his head. 'Beggin' your pardon, Mrs Treharne, but it's the truth!'

'We are greatly indebted to you, Mr Mahoney,' Alice told him. She leaned sideways in the saddle, kissing him lightly on his coal-smeared cheek. 'Be sure I shall not forget.'

'Me neither, ma'am. It surely was a pleasure.' Finn smiled up at her in that same moonstruck way they all did when they looked at Alice. He touched the place on his cheek like he didn't aim to wash it for the next month or so. 'Best get from here now, before they come lookin'.'

He darted off round the far side of the block, away from sight. From behind us I heard the reverend call out again.

'Ladies, I beg you!' He nudged his own mount forward, already starting clear of the jailhouse. 'There is no time to delay!'

'I hear you, Reverend,' I told him.

I set heels to the flanks of the bay

horse, and we took off flying. He was a good critter, the bay, kind of frisky at first with a new rider aboard, but once I talked gentle to him he steadied down. It was kind of a wrench to leave my roan horse back in Tylerville, to say nothing of the saddle that had cost me close on a hundred bucks, but I guess he'd have to keep. If things worked out, I'd be back. If not, either Finn or the folks at the stables would see him right.

Once we were away from town, into the brush and heading for the mountains, they started talking.

'We spoke to Mr Mahoney earlier,' Alice said. How she got to look that innocent I'll never know. 'He found us these horses, and devised a plan to draw attention from us while we made our escape.' She glanced my way questioningly. 'That was very kind of him, don't you think?'

'Sure, firin' Hildreth's place.' I shook my head. Reckon I was still recalling her performance in the jailhouse. 'That was one hell of a plan, all right. Wonder what brought that on, huh?'

She said nothing, bowing her head in its bonnet as angelic as you like.

'I must tell you, Miss Soledad, this goes sore against my principles.' The reverend seemed to bite out the words, flinching as the saddle jarred his backbone. 'It is not my way to break the law of God or man, and it comes hard for me to abandon my wagon in Tylerville with the mules and the tools of my trade. Nevertheless, my duty was plain. I could not leave you helpless in the tents of the Amalekites.'

'That's real nice of you, Reverend,' I told him. I meant it, too.

All the same, I kept my eye on the back trail as darkness dropped over the badlands and the three of us rode on. Don't know what the others thought, but I reckoned we still had Mulgrew to deal with. The old lawman wouldn't take kindly to losing his prisoner, and I got the feeling he wasn't about to let it lie. Sooner or later, that posse would be after us again.

I let out a breath, and rubbed my fingers around the inside of my shirt neck. Seemed like I could almost feel the rope, and those hemp fibres were starting to itch. We'd got clear of Mulgrew once, but staying ahead was likely to be even tougher.

I only hoped to hell that I was wrong.

7

We made it to Walleye not long after dawn broke.

To say it wasn't much to look at would be giving airs to the place. Walleye was a cluster of adobes and wood-framed shacks bunched together in a clearing cut out of the pine woods at the foot of the mountains. Half the tree stumps hadn't been grubbed up, and the trail wound around them, a ribbon of mud and dirt that grew into the main street. Tell truth, I didn't see any others. The shacks nearest the mine belched black smoke from holes in their roofs, and even at this hour the pounding of steam hammers was enough to send a man deaf. The shaft was sunk into the rock at the end of town, and ore wagons trundled back and forth on a rusted railtrack between it and the smoking buildings, hauled by a heavy rope on a windlass. In my time I reckon I've set eyes on some unlovely places, but Walleye was so bad it made Tylerville look close to refined. If I'd been travelling alone, one look would have been enough for me to turn my horse and ride all the way back. But I had Alice and the preacher with me, and there was no way we could turn tail now.

We'd dismounted halfway down the street, roping our mounts to the nearest rail, when we heard the hard, flat blast of the shot.

That sound cut through everything else like a knifeblade, and the drunks hurried to crawl off the street. Turning in the direction of the shot as its echoes died, I saw a bunch of *hombres* twenty yards off at the edge of the walk. Those nearest were rigged in heavy cord or wool pants and flannel shirts, and had to be miners. They'd arranged themselves in a half-circle and now it went backwards, opening up to show what was inside. Three hard-looking jaspers all toting pistols, and another feller stretched out in the mud, going nowhere.

'Now you seen it,' the first of the gunhawks said. Seemed to me he spoke real quiet, but his voice carried all the same. 'Cross Mr Webster, you know what to expect.'

He stood facing the miners, all of them looking mad enough to tear him apart. That smoking pistol he held was all that kept them back, I figured. Behind the gun there wasn't too much of him, a little *hombre* in workaday denims, the hat pulled low to shade his eyes. His face was thin and smooth, and I doubt he'd have weighed a hundred pounds wet through and with a grainsack round his neck, but he sure as hell had those miners scared. Seeing the man he'd just shot down, I guessed I knew why.

'You just stole his claim, goddammit!' a black-bearded miner yelled. It was as if he had to call out or bust. Right away, the little feller turned on him.

'You care to repeat that, mister?' the gunhawk asked.

His voice came out close to a whisper, but it cut the air keener than a razor would. At sound of it the miner swallowed and gulped. He didn't speak. Around him his friends scowled and muttered some, but they had nothing to say either. Behind the small man one of the other gunhawks chuckled, and spat into the mud.

'Let's go, Salinas,' this one said. 'These sons of bitches know when they're whipped.'

'They better.' Salinas blew down the smoking barrel, reset the hammer carefully. 'Just remember, do like we tell you, an' you get to stay healthy. Any trouble, I might just come lookin' again.'

He holstered his pistol and turned his back, stepping away down the walk with the other gunslingers in tow. The miners were still muttering and cursing when they saw us coming, and edged back to let us by.

The fallen man lay sprawled out in the mud, both hands flung wide like he was searching for a hold on something. He was dead all right. Salinas' bullet made a dark, neat hole in his flannel shirt just above the left breast, an outright killing shot. The *hombre*'s head was thrown back with his ragged beard jutting upward, and his eyes stared wide into ours. Halting by the body, I heard Alice gasp. Then the reverend stepped between us and the dead man, and picked the miner's hat from the ground to cover the face.

'Brethren, let us pray,' the reverend said. He stood up tall and straight and bowed his head, both hands gripping his hat to his chest. I tugged off my hat and ducked my head, and caught sight of some of the miners doing the same.

'Lord, pity this poor sinner gone to his account,' the reverend said. His voice boomed along the street, and folks peered out of their doors to see what went on. They didn't bother the reverend, and he just went ahead.

'Death has plucked him from this world in violence and pain, but all of us have sinned and fallen short of Thy glory. Yet we are all children of God. Amen.'

'Amen,' I said. It seemed like the thing to do. Halfway down the street Salinas and his friends turned back to look. The gunhawks laughed, and kept on walking.

'All children of God, huh?' I murmured.

'Thanks for the service, Reverend,' one of the miners offered. He signed to a couple of the others, who began to haul the dead man off the street. 'Sure do appreciate it.'

'A Christian duty, no more.' Reverend Hall bowed his grizzled head, slapping on his hat. He turned, stretching a long arm to include us both. 'Allow me to introduce my two companions. Mrs Treharne, Miss Soledad.'

He didn't need to trouble pointing Alice out to them. Most of the bearded men were already grinning shyly at the small blonde woman in her grey gown who stood, only a little paler than before, watching them drag the body away.

'Sure am glad to meet you, ma'am,' the spokesman said. He doffed his hat, glancing to the moonstruck crowd about him. 'Name's Bill Meredith, an' these here are some friends of mine.'

'We're here to confirm a claim.' Alice struggled with the words, her cheeks a shade less rosy than was usual. I guessed she didn't see men shot dead most days of the week. 'I'm truly sorry to trouble you at such a time, but we'd be grateful for directions to the appropriate office. I presume there is one here in Walleye?'

'That'll be Webster's place, ma'am,' Meredith said. He pointed to a building at the far end of the street. From here it looked bigger than the other ram-shackle efforts we could see. 'He has the claims an' assay office here. Was I you, though, I'd be mighty careful of him. He ain't a nice feller to know.'

'Damn right he ain't!' another man cut in, his face still hot with anger. 'Clancy, him that they're draggin' off the street here, he done staked his claim three weeks back, but them three bastards yonder — beggin' your pardon, lady — they just jumped it an' shot him down when he wouldn't back off. Same goes for all of us if we don't sell out to Webster real soon!'

'That's right,' Meredith said, and mutters of agreement came from the rest. Looking across to Alice, I saw the colour was back in her cheeks, and with it a fiercer light in her blue eyes that I'd come to know well by now. Usually, it meant trouble for me.

'Why, that's outrageous!' Alice had got back her sharp, schoolmarm voice, and it cut the silence like a quirt. 'This Mr Webster is nothing better than a common criminal, ready to use murderers to accomplish his evil purposes. Does Walleye have no law officer, a marshal or town constable?'

A few of them grinned at that, but

there wasn't too much enjoyment in it. Meredith shook his head, his bearded features almost apologetic.

'Not a one, ma'am.' He eyed the backs of the disappearing gunhawks, still wary. 'Some of us was thinkin' of formin' a vigilance committee. That was before Salinas and his bunch showed up, less than a month ago.'

'So this Webster has the place in his pocket.' The reverend spoke quietly, his weatherbeaten face grim behind the greying beard. 'How many of these ne'er-do-wells has he to call on?'

'A dozen or more,' Meredith told him. 'Most of 'em on the run from the Rangers. That's what we heard. Salinas, he's the worst, but they're all of 'em pretty mean. They've already killed three men who wouldn't give up their claims. Clancy here was just the last.'

'Most of us ain't in no hurry to join him, neither,' a fourth miner said.

To me, it sounded pretty reasonable. Alice, though, had her blood up now, and there was no way she aimed to go back.

'I am here to register a legitimate claim, on behalf of my departed husband,' she told the awestruck miners around her. Alice set back her shoulders and raised her head, those blue eyes blazing defiance. 'Dear Jim, God rest him, would not have had me turn tail at the first sign of danger. I shall go to see your Mr Webster, and I shall insist on what is due to me.'

She moved away smartly, hoisting her skirts ankle-high as she stepped through the mud and down the street towards Webster's place. For a moment the reverend and me stood staring after her, none too sure whether to follow her or not.

'Alice!' I called. Before the words came out, I knew I was wasting my time. 'Alice, hold on a minute! No way he's gonna talk to you!'

She didn't so much as turn around, keeping on straight ahead. Seemed like the two of us had no choice but to follow her.

Mr Webster's place was a wooden building, bigger than the other hovels further back, but nothing to write home about. It looked to me like a bunch of drunks had put it together, with slats and planks of different sizes, nailing them to the frame just as they pleased. Still, I guess Mr Webster must figure it suited him pretty good.

The pint-sized gunfighter they called Salinas was leaning up by the wall alongside the door, rolling himself a cigarette. His two shadows stood watching from further along the walk, hands on their pistols. Salinas firmed up his smoke and lit it, looking the three of us over as he flicked away the match. When we reached the door he eased himself in front, lowering his hand to rest on the gun-butt in his holster.

'An' just what in hell would you be wantin'?' Salinas asked.

'We're here to see Mr Webster, on

business,' Alice told him. She stepped up to face him, looking him as straight in the eye as his squint would allow. 'Now, if you would be so kind as to let us inside.'

'What kind of business, lady?' Salinas wanted to know. The tight sound in his voice made me more nervous than before. You could tell he didn't take kindly to Alice, and the fact she stood as tall as him wasn't helping his temper. That, and the other two gunhawks, who'd begun to grin and chuckle behind their hands at what they saw. 'Hurry it up now, I'm waitin'!'

You have to hand it to Alice. Faced by that mean little killer, she didn't so much as flinch. Just went forward, brushing past him as if he wasn't there.

'It's a personal matter, Mr Salinas,' she told him as she edged by him for the door. 'Now, if you will let us see him, we shall be most grateful.'

Salinas stood staring for an instant like he couldn't believe it. In that split second or so, me and the reverend stepped past him as Alice knocked on the door and went right in. Salinas called out to the other two gunslingers, and the three of them came in behind us, hauling out their pistols.

'It's all right, Salinas,' Webster said.

He sat behind the battered desk at the far side of the room, a kerosene lamp on a hook in the ceiling overhead lighting up the dark around him. The desk held a bunch of old ledgers, a pair of scales and a set of weights like I'd seen assayers use. Mr Webster, though, I never had seen before. If I had, you can be sure I'd have remembered him. I reckon he had to be one of the handsomest fellers I ever set eyes on, tall and slender and dark-complexioned, rigged in a grey Prince Albert coat and black pinstripe pants tucked into hand-tooled boots that right now rested on the desk top with the ledgers and the scales. If I'd met him any other place but this, that man would have had another conquest on his hands, I swear.

I was still studying him and figuring I couldn't get enough of what I saw, when I heard Alice call out from beside me like she'd just seen a ghost.

'Jim!' Her voice came out like a scream, echoing round the room. Alice broke into a fast, stumbling kind of run, making towards him. 'Jim Treharne! You're alive!'

Back in the doorway behind us, Salinas and the other gunmen froze, looking at each other and trying to figure out what was going on. From the frown on the face of the reverend, I could see he was none too happy either. Webster swung both feet off the desk and pushed out of his chair as Alice headed for him, moving so the desk stood between them.

'Easy, Alice.' He caught her arm as she darted around the desk, holding her away from him. 'I'm Mr Webster around here. They don't call me Treharne right now.'

'But, Jim.' Alice frowned, puzzled. She looked up questioningly into his face, still trying to take in what was happening. 'They told me you were dead.'

'Sure they did,' he sighed, a hint of anger in his voice. 'That's what everybody was supposed to think. Why the hell did you come here, Alice?'

He let go of her arm, walking back to the desk. Alice stood there watching him go. She had a stunned, beaten look that I'd never seen before. Right then I felt real sorry for her, I guess. Under all the toughness, it seemed like she could still be hurt bad. And Treharne, or Webster as he called himself, had hurt her all right.

'I came to check out the claim,' Alice was saying. She spoke dully, that stunned expression still on her face. 'Jim, aren't you pleased to see me? After all, you told me to follow you.'

'Not after they buried me, I didn't,' Treharne said.

A door opened behind him, and a woman came into the room. She was a big, plump-bosomed redhead and she

148

wasn't wearing nothing more than the flimsiest wrapper you ever saw, so those bosoms were well in view. When she saw Treharne and smiled, I swear I could see the paint and powder cracking on her cheeks, but she didn't appear to mind. She had her arms wrapped around him when she caught sight of Alice standing there, and the look she was sending her.

'So who's this prissed-up china doll?' the red-head asked. She eyed Alice up and down like someone had just thrown trash into the room. 'She lose her way or somethin'?'

Treharne didn't answer, disentangling himself the best way he could. I reckon he knew what was coming.

'Take your hands off my husband, you painted slut!' Alice shouted.

She came flying at the half-dressed female hung round Treharne's neck, and pulled her away from him. The pair of them went sprawling down, yelling and clawing and yanking at each other's hair. I have to say I was mighty impressed. Alice was well outmatched for size and weight, but she fought like a bobcat all the same. She had the other female down and was using her hair to slam her head against the floor, and you could hear the thudding of each blow on the dirt underneath them.

'Ladies! Ladies, please!' The reverend sounded shocked. He started towards the rolling heap of battling females and pulled up short, none too sure what to catch hold of first. Treharne, though, had had enough.

'Salinas!' he yelled to the gunmen in the doorway. 'Get in here!'

He grabbed Alice by one arm and dragged her clear of the redhead on the ground. She struggled and tried to break free of him, but Treharne was too strong for her. He handed her over to one of the gunhawks, who pinned both arms to her sides.

'Let her go at once!' the reverend boomed.

He dived in for them, his hands outstretched, but Salinas was faster.

The little *hombre* whacked his gunbarrel along the side of the preacher's head, and the reverend went down like he'd been poleaxed. Salinas stood off with the pistol levelled as Reverend Hall groaned and shook his head on the floor. With the third gunhawk's weapon pointing my way, I figured it was better not to make a move.

'You see what that bitch did to me?' the overstuffed female moaned. She got up from the dirt, the wrapper all but torn clean off her ample frame. Her hair was pulled and dragged all over her face, and tearstreaks and scratches showed through the paint. Treharne, though, didn't look too worried by it.

'Out of here, Red,' he told her. 'Later, maybe.'

The redhead snuffled something in answer, and went out through the back door, doing her best to hold what was left of the wrapper around her.

'You want me to finish him, boss?' Salinas asked. He stood over the reverend, holding the pistol like he couldn't wait to use it again. Back behind the desk, Jim Treharne shook his head.

'Leave him,' the tall feller said. 'He'll keep.' For the first time, he looked at me and what he saw appeared to interest him. 'So who are you, lady?'

'Name's Soledad, Mr Treharne,' I told him.

I met his look straight on as I answered. Tell truth, I couldn't take my eyes off the man. He was handsome, no doubt about it, his face shaved smooth but for a neat moustache, his black hair slicked back and those dark eyes burning into me like coals. Right now they were looking me up and down, and getting warmer. I might as well tell it straight, folks: when Vaughan Burrell gave me that kind of look, I hadn't cared for it one bit; when this *hombre* did it, I reckoned I didn't mind at all. Next minute, though, his glance had left me and was back with Alice again.

'Can't say I haven't been expecting you,' Treharne said. Now I listened to him closer, his voice had something of the same sound to it as Alice's had when I heard her first. Not that it should have been any surprise, both of them coming from Cornwall and all. 'I was hoping you might be persuaded to turn back, Alice, but it seems you never listen. And now it's too late.' He paused, glancing to the door behind him, and called out, 'OK, fellers, you can come in now.'

The door opened slowly, and this time it wasn't no blowsy redhead came in, but three men I'd come to know pretty well and hoped not to see again. They ranged themselves behind Treharne, smiling unpleasantly as Salinas and the others kept us covered from the far side of the room.

'Miss Soledad.' Vaughan Burrell touched his hat, eyes pale and cold as chips of stone. Either side of him Rufe Simmons and the undertaker, Hildreth, twisted their mouths to match him. 'And Mrs Treharne, too. This sure is a pleasure.'

'Wish I could say the same, Burrell,' I told him.

'Jim?' Alice stood, her bonnet hanging from her neck by its torn ribbons, her blonde hair falling across her flushed, tearful face. She looked to Treharne, her voice begging almost. 'Jim, please tell me what's happening here?'

'Kinda slow, ain't she?' Simmons muttered. The thick-set *hombre* laughed, the noise rumbling in his chest. A cold stare from Burrell quietened him again.

'Perhaps you'd better tell her, Jim,' Burrell said.

Treharne ignored him, still studying Alice and me as he spoke. 'It's quite simple, Alice,' Treharne said. 'Walleye is my town. Thanks to my friends here, I own the place now. Most of the claims have sold out to me and my partners, and the few that are left will be — encouraged — to do the same very soon. These mountains are made of silver, honey, and it's all in my pocket.'

'Saw some of your encouragin', back down the street,' I offered. I sensed a shift of movement from the gunhawks behind me, and wished I'd kept my mouth shut. Treharne, though, appeared not to have heard me, going right on.

'I run the claims, and the assay office, and I'm the only law in the place.' He gave a tight, impatient smile, shaking his head. 'Things would have been just fine if you'd taken the hint and gone back to St Louis, Alice. Burrell here tried to warn you off plenty of times already. But, as usual, you weren't listening.'

'But why should you want to leave me? Why change your name?' Alice was close to tears, her voice choking. She fought vainly against the *hombre* who held her, still staring at her husband as if he was going to make everything all right. Some hope, I thought.

'I told you already, I'm sitting on a fortune here.' Treharne cut the words back sharply, his patience running out.

'As for the change of name, there were a few things I didn't mention to you, back in St Louis. Like the little matter of fifteen thousand dollars I was obliged to draw on from a business syndicate there, and a number of gambling debts that remain unpaid. Thanks to Burrell and Hildreth here, my creditors will now believe me dead.'

'So where do they come into it?' I figured I knew the answer.

'Hildreth is an undertaker,' Treharne told me. 'Try working it out.'

'But we know the truth, Jim,' Alice said.

By now she'd swallowed back her sobs, dabbing her tears away. Alice crouched by the reverend, who groaned and touched a hand to the throbbing welt on his temple as he struggled to rise and fell back again. Above the fallen preacher her blue eyes met the darker ones of her husband. Now she was calm, the way a prisoner is when he looks at the judge and sees no mercy.

'That's right, Alice,' Treharne said.

'You know the truth. That's why I didn't want you here in Walleye, and now it's why you and your friends can never go back.' He signed to Salinas and the others, his voice hard and commanding. 'Get them out of here. In a while, I'll decide what's to be done.'

'May God forgive you, Jim,' Alice said.

The gunhawk who held her dragged her backwards for the door, and for once she didn't struggle, the fight gone out of her. The other gunman caught hold of Reverend Hall under the armpits and lugged him towards the doorway. Salinas stood a couple of feet clear of me, and jerked his pistol barrel to the door. I turned, heading back the way I'd come.

'Told you I'd see you die, you bitch,' Vaughan Burrell said.

'Not if I can help it, Burrell,' I told him.

'Spirited filly, ain't she?' Jim Treharne said. He smiled at me, those dark eyes running over me like the flame off a torch. 'Could be we'll keep her a little longer.'

I felt the gaze of those eyes touch and hold me fast. Maybe if I'd stuck around any longer, I might just have melted on the spot. But Salinas scowled and jerked his gun-barrel towards the open door, and I guessed I better not put him out right now. I broke the grip of Treharne's stare and stumbled out, but I reckon he knew he'd held me there.

Wake up, girl, I told myself. Get yourself a mite of sense. The sonofabitch is going to kill us all.

Sure, Soledad, I answered myself in my mind. And what the hell do we do about it?

Seemed like I couldn't find an answer for that one, no matter how I tried.

I headed out on to the street, hearing Salinas shut the door behind me.

8

'See what you mean 'bout that husband of yours, Alice,' I said.

The room they'd locked us into was on the back of the ramshackle building that passed for the saloon in these parts. The saloon itself was a miserable dive that wouldn't have cost Finn Mahoney a minute's sleep, and the back room was even worse. I reckon they might have made a half-decent broom closet out of the place if they worked at it real hard, but from what I'd seen Walleye wasn't a place that attracted workers, unless you counted the dumb suckers burrowing in the mines. I sat backed up to the wall, close to the locked door, my knees drawn up against my chin. If I stooped low I could almost stand upright. A tall feller like the reverend spent most of his time bent double, or crouching on his haunches. He and

Alice hunkered side by side, the far wall against their backs. I figured if I measured it out, there might just be a couple of feet of open space between the three of us. Now Alice heard me, and raised her head.

'I'm sure I don't know what you mean,' she said. That waspish little sting in her voice warned me, but maybe I was past caring.

'Sure is one hell of a looker, ain't he?' I offered. Catching the fierce look she gave me, I shrugged and spread my hands. 'Well, no use sayin' he ain't, Alice. It's like a good horse, there's beauty there an' you got to admire it.' Now it was the turn of the preacher to frown disapprovingly across to me, and I knew it was time to quit. 'OK, Reverend. Handsome is as handsome does, I ain't forgotten that.'

'I'll thank you not to mention his name again,' Alice said, and there wasn't a pinch of friendliness in her voice. She turned from me to the reverend. 'Is he really going to kill us, do you think?'

'I believe that is his intention, my dear,' the preacher told her. 'Much as I wish myself mistaken, I know he means us no good.' He glanced up, meeting her gaze, and I saw there were tears in his eyes. 'For myself I do not mind so much, but to think of you and your friend, young women with your lives before you, suffering in this way. It is more than I can bear.'

He hauled out a square of cloth that would have done service for a flag, and blew his nose loudly. Alice leaned over and patted his hand.

'Don't you take on, Mr Hall.' Her voice had softened in a moment. 'We are not dead yet.'

'If we don't get out of here, we soon will be,' I said.

They'd left the one slop bucket between the three of us, and by now it had begun to smell kind of ripe. The flies that came to it were giving us hell, too. Being a gentleman, Reverend Hall had rigged up a makeshift screen with his coat and a line of rawhide cord fixed to a hook in the wall, and when we used the bucket he'd turn his back. Only trouble was, they'd bored a spyhole in the door, and whoever was on guard kept peering through every once in a while. Still, it beat being dead. Just about.

And then, while Alice comforted the reverend and I kept slapping the flies away, I knew what I had to do. It was like the sun burst through a bank of cloud and dazzled me blind, and in spite of the room and the bucket I caught myself smiling. Edging over to the door, I stared through the spyhole at a bloodshot eye looking the other way.

'Get me out of here, goddammit!' I hollered. I hammered on the door, so hard the wood rattled against the lock. 'Let me out, you hear? I got to talk to Webster!'

I felt the floor move as Alice and the preacher turned around, glimpsed their shocked faces as my shouting froze them for an instant. I paid no mind, battering that door until it creaked and groaned for mercy. After a while, the eye found a voice.

'OK, OK. Take it easy!' That was Rufe Simmons yelling back at me. 'You want to see him, come ahead, but you're gonna be mighty sorry.'

The key rasped in the lock, and the door squealed and shuddered open. Simmons bent double outside, framed in greyish light as he lined the big Remington pistol on what was inside. Seeing me there, he scowled and edged back, beckoning me out.

'Hurry it up, bitch,' Simmons called. From here he looked more like a grizzly than ever, and the ugliest of the breed at that. 'I ain't here to wait around!'

No, I know what you're here for, I thought. I didn't tell him, though, just scuttled out of that stinking place as fast as I could make it. Behind me I heard Alice cry out angrily, and the murmured voice of the reverend trying

163

to calm her down.

'You damn traitor, Soledad!' Alice yelled. 'I'll never forgive you for this!'

Her voice came after me through the door as Simmons slammed it and turned the key in the lock. The sound cut me inside like a lash from a blacksnake whip, and I reckon my eyes might have watered just a little, knowing what she was thinking. Right now, though, I had no time to stay worried about it. Simmons gripped my arm so hard you could hear the muscles moan, and was shoving me across the saloon for the doors that led on to the street. A few of the drinkers looked up from their rotgut snakehead or whatever they were using to poison themselves with, but nobody tried stopping us. With Simmons hauling me along, I figured that had to make sense. A few seconds later we shoved back the rickety doors and stepped into the street.

Treharne was across the far side of

the muddy track, one of the gunmen with him. For once, he didn't hold my eye the longest. For a while, all I saw was the horse.

I got to tell you, I ain't never seen nothing like him. Not even that palomino stud I had comes close. He was a big grey stallion, smooth and silvery as the finish on a pistol barrel, and the muscles sliding under his skin like silk. He was shying and bucking as he fought the halter-rope, trying to pull free of the gunhawk who held it. I stood staring, taking in that smooth line of neck and back and haunch as he snorted and flung his mane, glaring from his fierce black eyes. He had to be the most beautiful horse I'd ever seen in my life, and the meanest.

'Hold him still, goddammit!' Treharne shouted. He came in close as the gunman dragged the stallion down on all four hooves, and caught hold of the saddle they'd fitted on. How they did that I'll never know. 'I'm getting on him now!'

'He ain't ready to be ridden, Mr Webster.' The gunhawk bit the words through his teeth, both heels digging dirt as the big grey fought to heave up again. Treharne didn't answer, grabbing the saddlehorn to swing himself astride and snatching up the rein. I could have told him he was wasting his time, and risking his neck into the bargain. As horsemen went, he was passable enough, but a bronc-buster would have had trouble with that critter. Treharne hung tight as the stallion bucked and wheeled in a circle in the middle of the street, lashing the horse across its nose with the short quirt he was carrying. The stallion straightened out, still bucking hard, and Treharne dug his spurs. It wasn't a smart thing to do. The grey pulled up short like he'd hit a wall, and Jim Treharne shot over his head and into the mud, water and filth spraying up as he landed.

The big grey kicked out with his hind legs and swung away, heading down the street. Now and then he shied and threw up his head against the rope that dragged on the ground. The gunman had dived clear on to the walk and Rufe Simmons stood like he'd been turned to stone. Nothing for it, I guessed. I stuck fingers to my lips and whistled, hard and shrill as I could. Then again, and again, until that stallion halted and turned, looking back to me.

'Over here, feller!' I called to him. I stepped out on the mud, looking him in the eye and keeping my voice low and gentle. 'Come on, feller, this way!'

He stood glaring at me a while, blowing hard down his nose. Then the grey came forward, heading to me. I didn't move now, letting him come, and still talking. 'That's it, feller,' I told him. 'That's the way. Come ahead, I'm waitin'.'

The stallion kept coming on forward, pausing to stamp and fight the dangling rope once in a while. Pretty soon he was about as close as I wanted him to be, black eyes blazing down as he shook that glossy mane and flared his nostrils at me.

'That's just fine, feller,' I said. I put just as much warm feeling into the words as I could muster. 'That's a real good horse.'

I bent down, real slow, and gathered up the rope. He reared up at that, slashing down with those sharp hooves in the mud, but I kept on talking until he stood quiet again. The gunhawk came alongside, breathing hard, and took the rope from me.

'Get him out of here,' I said. 'Ain't nobody gonna ride that horse today.'

Treharne struggled up out of the dirt. His grey Prince Albert and starched shirt were splashed and filthy with the wet mud from the street, his features smeared and sweating. He had that quirt gripped tight in his hand, and for a while he looked ready to kill. Then he took a breath and simmered down.

'Do like she says,' he told the other man. 'I'll deal with that bastard later.'

The gunman nodded. He led the

stallion off, still battling against the rope and stamping as it went. I watched that horse as long as I dared, but pretty soon Treharne had all my attention.

'So what the hell are you doing here?' he asked.

'She wanted to see you, Mr Webster.' Simmons came alive at last, speaking for me.

'Is that right?' Treharne still sounded mean. His dark eyes blazed at me like the horse's had done, and I figured just how akin the two of them were. 'What for?'

'That's a mighty fine horse you have there, Mr Webster,' I said. I reckoned it might help to change the subject. 'Where'd you get him?'

'None of your damn business!' he blazed back. Then the mood altered and he shrugged, that easy smile returning. 'All right, Soledad. You'd better come with me.'

He clambered up on to the walk, and led me to his place. Once we got there he ushered me inside and left Rufe on

169

the walk, shutting the door on him.

'So you wanted to see me, lady?' Treharne settled back in that same chair, his feet up on the desk with its ledgers and scales. Even bruised and splashed with mud, he was still handsome as hell, that smile breaking out like afternoon sunshine and his eyes burning holes in my conscience. 'What is it you want from me?'

'I recalled what you said, last time I was here,' I told him. 'You said maybe you'd save me for later.'

'And what if I did?' Treharne was relaxed now, smiling like a cat. His warm eyes raked me up and down, studying the denim shirt and cords. 'You always wear that rig, lady?'

'You ever try bronc-busting in a dress?' I wanted to know.

He laughed at that, shaking his handsome head as he looked me over. 'I suppose not,' Treharne allowed. 'So, what can I do for you, Soledad?'

'I thought while you were saving me, you might see your way to saving Alice and the Reverend,' I said.

'And why the hell should I do that?' All at once the smile was kind of tight.

'I get the feelin' you wouldn't want Alice dead,' I told him.

Jim Treharne swung his legs off the desk, the chair creaking as he shoved it back.

'Damn it, I didn't want her here at all!' Treharne shouted. He slammed his fist on the desk top so that the scales jangled and shivered. 'Why in hell did she follow me to Walleye?' He threw himself back in the chair, breathing hard. 'No way I can let her go, or you either.'

'No need to have us killed,' I offered. 'We wouldn't be any trouble. An' even if you were to let us go, I'd make sure none of us talked about it.'

'The reverend too?' Treharne sounded none too sure.

'I reckon I could do it. He's awful fond of Alice.'

'Yes.' His voice had a cold, unforgiving sound. 'I noticed that.' Treharne sat straight, slapping his hand on the desk like he'd swatted away a fly. 'I can make sure no one talks, Soledad. I can have you all killed. Burrell would do it, he'd like to see you dead.'

'Reckon I feel just the same towards him, Mr Webster.'

'Hildreth, too. That little son was fit to be tied when you burned his funeral parlour.' Treharne chuckled, his smile turning cruel. 'So, Soledad. What's the deal? If I do as you ask, and let you live, what can I expect to gain?'

I looked into those dark, searing eyes, and took a breath. 'I'm the best when it comes to horses,' I said. All the time I tried to hide the shake in my voice. 'Ain't nobody in Walleye can handle 'em like I do, an' that's somethin' you can always use. Besides, I already done you one favour back there on the street.'

'Catching up the horse, you mean?'

'Not just that; gettin' the other feller to take him away.' I stared him straight in the eye, and this time I meant it. 'If

I'd left you to ride him again, that critter would've killed you, Mr Webster. Try it again, he just might do it yet.'

'Is that so?' He brushed at the mud on his face, frowning for a moment. Jim Treharne got to his feet, easing around the desk towards me. 'Maybe I do owe you a favour, at that, Soledad. But I wasn't thinking about the horses.'

Now I was into deep water, right enough. He was up close, his arm on my shoulder. The smile was back at his lips, and his gaze burned into me hot as a furnace. I held him off, but it sure wasn't easy, I can tell you.

'As I remember, you got a woman,' I said.

'Red, you mean?' He laughed, slipping his arm about my waist and pulling me closer. 'I can have any woman I like in Walleye, Soledad. Now you, you're different. You're not like the rest, and that's what I want. And the name's Jim, not Mr Webster.'

He brought his lips down on mine then, and it was something all right. He kissed just as good as he looked. It would have been easy to go along with him, too, and I guess that any other time I might just have lain down and finished business then and there. But someplace at the back of my mind I saw Alice and the reverend, and remembered how they'd got me out of jail in Tylerville. I knew I had to stick by them, and see they got out of here with their lives. And for their sake, I couldn't give him what he wanted.

Don't think it didn't cross my mind, though.

Treharne was kissing me like he didn't want it to stop. I figured I didn't either, and that was warning enough. I broke free of him, standing clear.

'Maybe this ain't the time, Jim,' I said.

He caught the flushed, breathless state of me, and smiled like he knew it all.

'You think so?' Treharne leaned back against the desk, getting his breath. 'Perhaps you're right, Soledad. I still have business to attend to, I daresay.' He smiled again, torching me with his eyes. 'Tell you what, have Simmons bring you back here tonight. Maybe we can work something out.'

'Sure, Jim. I'll do that,' I said.

I was still trying to breathe slower, and my heart was slapping on my ribs, as Simmons took me back across the street.

Alice and the reverend were waiting for me, and neither of them looked too friendly. The key had barely turned in the lock before it started.

'I take it you enjoyed your *tête-à-tête* with my husband?' Alice's voice stung so sharply I could feel the poison in my blood. The hate that filled her blue eyes was hard to bear. She wasn't dumb, and guessing what she did you couldn't blame her. 'What kind of arrangement did you come to, if it isn't too much to ask?'

'He wants me to go back there tonight,' I said.

I wasn't dumb, either, and I knew

what was coming. Alice flew at me like a wildcat, slashing with her nails and trying to grab my hair. She was spirited, all right, and pretty strong for a woman of her size, but this time it was different. I wasn't Red, and I'd handled tougher than Alice in my time. Seemed like it wasn't too long before I had her down and was sitting astride her, pinning her arms to the ground, while the reverend tutted and begged me to let her loose.

'Listen to me, Alice,' I said. I put my face as near as I dared, keeping my voice low so whoever was at the spyhole didn't hear. 'What I done back there was buy us a little time, that's all. Way I see it, we have to get out of here tonight, an' if we do it right, maybe we have a chance.'

'You're sure you don't want to stay behind?' Alice spat, thrashing around as she tried to throw me off. I sat tight, and waited for her to settle down.

'Nothin' happened back there, Alice,' I told her. 'Sure, it might have, but it didn't, an' that's the truth.' I waited until the reverend came closer, bending low to listen. 'Once we're out, Reverend, I want you to find Meredith an' some of his friends. Have 'em ready to fight, because I reckon me an' Alice will be comin' back. Mulgrew's out there someplace, an' I'd bet money he's ready to ride in here if he thinks it'll work.'

'I hear you,' the preacher said. He nodded down to the flushed, angry face of Alice. 'Let her up, Soledad.'

'Just don't scratch my eyes out, huh?' I said.

I let go her wrists and got off her, and Alice scrambled up. She glared at me as she straightened her rumpled gown and put her tousled hair to rights. From what I could see, she still wasn't too sure.

'Ain't sayin' it's gonna work, Alice,' I said. I hunched up by the wall, knees to my chin. 'It's our only chance, is all.' I paused, lowering my voice a couple of notches. 'You still have that stingy gun hid?'

Meeting my eyes, she nodded. They hadn't searched Alice too close, which was kind of dumb when you think about it. But then, most folks acted dumb when it came to Alice. Now she looked at me, not trusting, but a mite less unfriendly than before.

'Now hear me out,' I told them. 'This is what we'll do.'

They listened as I told it, keeping my voice to a whisper. At first Alice wasn't too eager, but after a while they nodded, and the three of us settled back. I don't know what they were thinking about as we waited for nightfall, but my mind was filled with Jim Treharne, and that handsome horse he'd tried to ride and failed.

Both of them beautiful, both of them mean as sin. That horse was so fine he had me dazzled, but I wouldn't have laid a hand to him. And while I'd been more than ready to lay a hand to Jim Treharne, I knew he couldn't be trusted. I'd stalled him for a few hours at most. After tonight,

I wouldn't be able to count on anything. And that was why I didn't aim to stay to find out.

I huddled against the wall, and waited for the night.

9

I was smothering in darkness that pressed on me like a heavy, stinking horse-blanket until I could hardly breathe. Someplace further off there was a war being fought, and a jackhammer was pounding against my skull. I opened my eyes and the same dark met me, broken only by a faint spill of light from under the door. I was in that broomcloset of a room with Alice and the preacher, and the shouting and yelling was from the drinkers in the saloon beyond. The pounding that threatened to shake the door off its hinges was coming from outside, and now I heard Rufe Simmons' voice.

'Wake up, goddammit!' the big grizzly shouted. 'Mr Webster's waitin', an' we ain't got all night!'

The key scraped into the lock, and

the door groaned open. Yellow lamp-light came flooding in, dazzling us for a moment, and I made out the bulky frame of Simmons standing there, the Remington pistol aimed and ready. Further inside the room, behind me, Alice moaned and clutched her belly, crouching on the ground.

'Help me, I'm sick,' Alice murmured. She looked to the stooped figure of the preacher, her eyes wide and pleading. 'Please, Reverend, get your coat. I have to use the bucket.'

She doubled over, retching like she was about to throw up, and hitched her skirts high enough to take Simmons' interest. Not that he needed too much inviting. As performances went, it wasn't half bad, and Simmons was right on cue. The minute Alice crouched over the pail and the reverend hoisted his coat, the big grizzly barged his way in, shoving the preacher aside for a closer look.

'Now this I got to see,' Rufe Simmons said, and that ugly grin carved his stubbled face from ear to ear. That's right, he was that bad. I edged around behind him as he moved in closer, ducking his head under the low ceiling. And then Alice turned around.

'Was this what you were looking for, Mr Simmons?' she asked. She had the twin-barrel derringer out of her bosom, and the pistol was lined on the middle of his face. 'Now drop the gun,' Alice said, her voice hard and chill as a pebble skimming a frozen pond. 'If not, I shall take great pleasure in blowing that grin from your face.'

Simmons tried to answer and choked on his words, staring down the barrel. Getting low behind him, I drove a booted foot into the back of his leg, grabbing at his shirt to haul him backwards. Simmons yelled and lurched but he didn't fall, still holding on to the Remington as he clawed at me with his free hand. The swing caught me across the side of the head and I went down hard, grunting as the floor came up to hit me. Then the reverend was in on Simmons, beating his gun-arm down.

'You despicable scoundrel!' the preacher said. One clenched fist hammered Simmons' forearm, dashing the pistol from his hold. The other swung in a full-blooded hook to that stubble-crusted jaw. For a reverend, he could punch all right. I heard the thud his calloused fist made as it landed, Simmons' bitten grunt as he reeled and fell. I got out from under, snatching up the fallen pistol as he crashed to earth. Alice was still holding the derringer, waiting the chance of a shot. The reverend had the key from the inside of the door and we were set to leave when Rufe Simmons heaved himself up again, grabbing at my leg to haul me down.

'Got you now, you goddamn bitch!' Simmons growled.

I felt his free hand lock like a vice on the back of my neck, and got ready to meet St Peter. Then this deafening clang shivered round the room like someone just hit a mission bell with a mallet, and Simmons sighed and collapsed, rolling away from me. Alice had slugged the big lunk with the slop pail, and as she let go the whole stinking works upended itself all over him. By then he was out cold and didn't care, but I'm telling you it couldn't have happened to a nicer feller.

'Nice work, Alice,' I said. It hadn't been a part of the plan, but it had worked out pretty good. Taking a risk with the mess he was in, I rifled Simmons' pockets and came up with a handful of shells. By then the reverend had the door open and the three of us were out of there, into the saloon.

The place was crowded, and most of the drinkers were so loud with their singing and bawling I doubt they heard a thing. I saw the bunch of *hombres* at the bar turn their heads mighty quick as we stumbled out into the light, and the hint in some of their faces that the owners were about to reach for their guns. I had the Remington up and levelled, using my free hand to dog back the hammer. At the sight of the pistol, and Alice with the derringer up alongside, they thought better of it.

'Guns on the floor!' I yelled. 'An' get clear, all of you! We're comin' through!'

Pistols came thudding out on the dirt floor, and the crowd went back and away to both sides like the parting of the waters. I caught sight of Burrell and Hildreth and their friends Brocklehurst and Ashman up by the bar, read the shock in their faces. I might have spared a word for the four of them, but right now I figured I didn't have the time.

'Let's go!' I shouted. I ploughed across the room, kicking pistols away as I made for the door. Back of me Alice grabbed up another weapon, and I glimpsed the reverend with a gun in both his hands. The .44 Remington was big and heavy enough for me to handle, and I didn't stop for anything else. Alice and me battered out through the doors, with the reverend backing out behind us, and we hit the street.

'Go find Meredith!' I yelled to the preacher. 'We'll catch ourselves some horses!'

The reverend needed no telling. He was away round the corner of the block and into the alleys before I'd finished shouting. There were plenty of horses to pick from, tethered at the hitching-rails. I chose the two nearest, loosened off the ropes and helped Alice into the saddle before mounting up myself.

We were clear of Walleye and into open country before an elf owl could blink its eye. Checking the horse I rode, I saw a lariat hung on the horn and a carbine fixed in a leather scabbard. It looked to me like an old US Army Springfield, single-shot. Alice had her two pistols, and that was all.

Out into the brush the dark was heavy and thick, long shadows hiding pits and hummocks in the trail. Pretty soon, I knew, we'd have to slow down if we didn't want our mounts to break a leg. It was then I glanced back over my shoulder and saw the horsemen coming after us.

'Three of 'em, Alice!' I shouted. At this distance I couldn't make out who they were, but I hoped to hell it wasn't Salinas. 'We have to find cover!'

I drove my horse forward, peering into the dark for anything that showed. After a while the mouth of a gully loomed ahead, littered either side with brush and boulders. I made for it at a run, praying the critter under me didn't find any gopher holes. The three *hombres* behind us were already a way closer by the time we gained cover.

'Head further up the gully and dismount!' I called to Alice. 'You stop 'em gettin' by, I'll take 'em from the side!'

I saw her gallop on down the gully, and knew she'd heard me. I slowed my own horse and climbed down, grabbed the lariat and the carbine, and slapped the animal's rump to send it after her. Once down, I dived into the nearest clump of boulders, laid the carbine down and started building a loop with the rope.

The three horsemen weren't far behind. I heard them slow up at the mouth of the gully, like they were thinking it over. Then I heard their voices.

'What you reckon, Burrell?' Jake Brocklehurst asked. He didn't sound too sure.

'What's the matter, Jake? You nervous, or something?' Burrell's voice was angry and mean. He wasn't any too pleased, you could tell. 'Two women, that's all. Only one can use a gun, an' there's three of us. Come on, they ain't gone far!'

'I'm with you, Burrell,' Kirk Ashman muttered.

Listening to them as I began to swing the lariat, I figured it made sense. Treharne wouldn't risk Salinas and the others tonight, when he might need them by him in town. Burrell had let us get away once already, and now we'd got past him again. The way Treharne saw it, it would be Burrell's job to bring us back. And that suited me just fine.

They entered the gully at a steady walk, building to a lope as they scoured the darkness. I let them pass, then came up on my feet and swung the loop. Kirk Ashman was furthest back, and he was the tallest. That made him the easiest target. The rope dropped neatly over his shoulders and I dug in and pulled before he could move. The noose plucked him out of the saddle and he hit the dirt with a solid thump, staying down. I was back behind the boulder as the other two wheeled around and fired, their bullets spitting into the rocks below me. The carbine was ready to hand and I lay flat, lining on the riders from cover. It was a Springfield like I thought, one shot but mighty accurate. I aimed above the head of Brocklehurst's mount and pressed the trigger. The bullet tore past the animal's ear like an angry hornet and the flat whiplash crack of the shot sent it bucking and shying like a regular rodeo terror. Jake Brocklehurst pitched out of his stirrups and slammed into the gully bed. He rolled over and sat up, moaning and holding his shoulder.

'Help me, Burrell!' he bawled. 'The goddamn thing's busted!'

'You still want to fight, Burrell!' I shouted. I edged out from cover with the .44 Remington levelled on him. 'Come ahead, I'm waitin'!'

He took one look and turned his mount, digging his spurs to make a break further along the gully. He hadn't gone far when Alice stepped out from a tumble of rocks, holding a pistol in either hand.

'Step down, if you please, Mr Burrell,' Alice said. She smiled brightly behind the levelled guns. 'Unless you'd rather I shot you dead, of course.'

Burrell looked into her face, and swallowed. He threw his pistol away from him, and climbed down shakily from his horse. I came down to join them, checking on the others. Brocklehurst was still moaning and rocking backwards and forwards, gripping his shoulder, and Ashman was sleeping soundly. I slackened off the lariat, and took it off him.

'Reckon you an' me got business to attend to, Mr Burrell,' I said.

'What do you mean?' Burrell asked. For once, his voice quavered. Dark as it was, I sensed the high colour drain from his round, pale-eyed face, leaving it flour-white against the night.

'You know what I'm talkin' about,' I said. I kicked the pistols of Ashman and Brocklehurst into the mesquite, and jabbed the Remington into his ribs. 'Now head on up the gully, an' make it fast.'

Alice fell in beside me and the pair of us marched him up the gully until we found a stunted piñon growing out of the brush on the near-side slope. Once we got there, I signalled him to halt.

'Unbuckle that belt, an' hand it over!' I ordered. 'An' don't be too long about it, or I just might shoot instead.'

He stared at me like I'd lost my mind,

and I could see him think about arguing the point. The Remington, and the mean expression I was wearing convinced him otherwise. Vaughan Burrell slacked off the belt and threw it over, grabbing hurriedly at his pants as they started to slide.

'Soledad, what are you doing?' Alice laughed helplessly, one hand to her mouth.

'Just keep that derringer on him, an' shoot if he makes a move,' I told her. I picked up the belt, stowing the Remington for the moment, and moved in to where Burrell stood waiting. 'Now, up against the tree, an' hold out your hands.'

'Like hell I will!' he burst out. Alice cocked her gun carefully, and he swore, stretching out both hands. I tied them tightly with his belt, fixing the other end to the tree as his breeches sagged again. Once he was fast I hauled them down to his ankles, and after that his long underwear. Pretty soon he was naked as a jaybird below the waist.

'Damn you, you can't do this to me!' Burrell yelled. Behind me Alice was doubled over, choking with laughter, but I didn't smile.

'Don't worry,' I told him, 'you ain't showed me nothin' a horse can't better. Now I got some questions for you, Burrell, an' you'd better answer me, you hear?'

'Ain't about to tell you nothing!' Burrell gritted, fury in his voice.

'We'll see.' I stood back a couple of paces, and coiled the lariat until it was the size of a fair-sized quirt. 'You figured me for a sucker in Tylerville, didn't you? Bought the horses from me, then tried to get the money back by cheatin' at cards. That's right, ain't it?'

'Go to hell,' Burrell answered, and I nodded.

'Have it your way,' I said.

I swung the lariat with all the strength and mean feeling that was in me, catching him a whipping blow across the butt. Burrell gasped and bit his lip, but stayed dumb. By now I guess my blood was up and I let him have it, slashing at that round behind that showed full and pale against the dark. After three or four he hollered out.

'OK, OK,' Burrell yelled. 'Sure it's right, you know that.'

'I needed to hear you say it.' I eased off, lowering my arm as Alice looked on wide-eyed from a distance. 'An' when that didn't work, you tried to get me hung for a horse-thief, didn't you? Your pals back there doctored my brand with a running iron an' claimed it was theirs. You were behind it, Burrell. Let me hear it.'

'Try provin' it.' He still had some fight left in him, and that fired me up again. I cut that rope across his ass like I was taking a sickle to grain. This time he cried out as it stung him, sobbing for breath.

'All right, goddammit.' His voice had gone a notch higher than before. 'I did it.'

'If that ain't horse-theft, it's somethin' mighty close,' I said. 'You'll go to jail, Burrell, an' you'll be lucky it ain't no worse than that. Then there's the business of Alice here. You knew she was comin', an' you aimed to stop her reaching Walleye, you an' Hildreth an' Simmons. Right?'

I lifted the coiled rope and he nodded, fighting to speak.

'Sure, that was us, and you know it.'

'Yeah.' I pondered on that, resting the lariat against my shoulder. 'That would be on account of your little arrangement with Jim Treharne, I reckon. There's plenty you can tell me about that, an' I ain't heard it yet. How'd you get in with him, for one?'

'Why don't you mind your business, bitch?' Vaughan Burrell muttered.

It wasn't what I cared to hear from a man who'd tried to get me hanged, and my temper flared up good and hot. I must have caught him six or seven licks with the rope, and long before I finished he was howling and

195

whimpering for me to quit.

'OK, I've had enough!' Burrell yelled. 'My butt feels like it's on fire, damn it!'

'You won't sit down easy for a while, that's for sure,' I told him. 'Now, about Treharne; you were saying?'

'We had word from the syndicate in St Louis, we got contacts there.' Seemed like he couldn't talk fast enough now. Sweat stood out on his brow, tears of pain and rage welling in his eyes. 'What Hildreth and me needed was somebody to take over Walleye and run it for us. Once they'd hit the silver lode, there were fortunes to be made, and we wouldn't need to lift a finger.'

'So you fixed the death, an' the burial,' I said.

'Sure, that was easy. Treharne staged a collapse on the street, and we got him clear.' Burrell's voice choked on a sob as he flinched at the pain of his whipped backside. 'Hildreth arranged the funeral, the coffin was full of stones and dirt. Treharne we got away inside a wagon and into Walleye. Long as we knew the truth, he had to give us our cut.'

'But then he brought the gunmen in, an' ran it for himself. That right?'

'You know it's right, damn you!' Burrell shot back. 'Sure, he's the big wheel now, but he still needs us, and we still get our share. So what the hell if you heard it from me now? No way you'll prove it!'

He broke off, whimpering and sobbing like a whipped kid. By now, I guess my temper was played out, and I began to feel a little sorry for him.

'That's all I needed to know, Burrell,' I said.

'That's right,' the other voice spoke from somewhere above my head. 'Reckon we've all of us heard enough now, Burrell.'

I peered into the darkness and saw Sheriff Mulgrew sitting his horse at the top of the slope behind me. Further back were the mounted figures of other riders, maybe as many as twenty or more. Boone Kennedy and the other young deputy were among them and, as I looked, the whole bunch of them started their horses down at a walk for the gully bed. I let go of the rope, dropping it into the trail as they reached us.

'Seems like I had you wrong, Miss Soledad,' Mulgrew said. He glanced to where Ashman and Brocklehurst sprawled in the dirt further off, and nodded. 'You an' Mrs Treharne here just done us a favour, I reckon. So where's the preacher?'

'Back in Walleye.' Alice spoke now, worry in her voice. 'He stayed behind to muster the miners after we escaped. They imprisoned us there, we were going to be killed.'

'This your husband, ma'am? The one we been hearin' about?'

Alice swallowed and fell silent, and I had to answer for her.

'Sure,' I told Mulgrew. 'Him, an' maybe a dozen gunfighters he's brought in to keep the town under. The reverend is rousing the miners to fight, but we're countin' on you to help. If you don't go in, those boys will be gunned down.'

'Ain't too sure 'bout that,' the oldster pondered, stroking his bristled jaw. 'It's over the county line.'

'So who's lookin'?' I demanded. 'There's folks in danger there, one of 'em a friend of ours. You go in now, Sheriff, people in Walleye are gonna thank you.'

'Uhuh.' Mulgrew frowned, and tugged at his heavy moustaches. 'If I do like you say, we better do it right. No sense goin' in like a cavalry charge an' killin' innocent folk. You got any ideas about that, lady?'

'Most of his killers are down by his place, or in the saloon,' I told him. 'Saloon's right side of the one street there, you can't miss it. Treharne's place is down at the far end, left side, biggest building on the street.'

'Please hurry, Sheriff,' Alice said. She looked up at him, eyes pleading.

'OK, you convinced me.' Mulgrew

turned, calling out to the men around him. 'Boone, George, bring them two fellers over here an' git 'em roped. Burrell can stay where he's at for now. Once you done that, git ready to ride. We got work to do.'

I caught up my horse and set foot to the stirrup, climbing into the saddle.

'Just a minute, lady!' Mulgrew sounded puzzled. 'Where the hell you goin'?'

'Best I go on ahead, Sheriff.' I cut the words back over my shoulder, already starting back along the gully. 'If this works, it oughta help you, I reckon.'

I heard his shouted protests, but paid them no mind. The last one I listened to was Alice as she called out to me.

'Soledad!' Her voice came after me down the gully. 'Soledad, you be careful!'

Hearing the fear in the words, I smiled. Seemed we were friends again, at that.

'You bet I will, Alice,' I said.

I tapped heels to the flanks of my

mount, urging it forward for the gully mouth. Way I saw it, I had business of my own to settle, back in Walleye.

★ ★ ★

When I reached the town again the night was fading, darkness ebbing away as a greyish half-light threatened in the sky. I made a detour through the rocks and brush, coming in along the backs of the buildings on the left side of the street. Those damned hammers still pounded away like the bells of hell, and wagons rattled in and out of the mineshaft, but I didn't pay too much attention. They covered the noise of my horse's hooves as it picked its way through the litter of rubbish thrown out behind the clapboard shacks. There was some noise on the street, but from the sound of it things were settling back down again. Treharne must have figured that even Burrell could catch two women, and he wouldn't be looking for me to come back alone.

I sure hoped not, anyhow.

I made it to the back of his place, and got down from the horse, roping him to a thorn bush that stood close. Tugging Simmons' pistol from my belt, I edged up to the back wall, and looked the building over. Rear of the place was solid, with no way in, but around the side was a small window that was screened by a tarpaper blind. I slid around the corner and up to the ledge, and hauled myself up and over the sill, trying not to make too much noise and hoping Salinas wasn't on the prowl. Last thing I wanted was to meet up with him again.

The window was a tight fit, and for a while I thought I wouldn't make it. Then the weight of my body took me through and I slid headfirst into the room. It looked to be some kind of storage place, filled with crates and sacks. Some of them weren't fastened down yet, and I caught the gleam of coins and bar silver in the crates. Looked like Walleye was a fortune waiting to be made, all right. I was up on my feet the moment I landed, the .44 Remington held out in front. Up ahead of me a door showed against the gloom, and a yellow bar of light beamed from beneath it. I turned the handle, and stepped inside.

Jim Treharne was standing by a larger window that gave a view of the street, his back towards me. At the sound of the opening door he turned quickly, just in time to look down the barrel of the pistol I was pointing his way.

'Soledad.' The surprised look lasted only for an instant, replaced at once by that warm, knowing smile. 'What brings you back so soon?'

'Over to the chair, Jim, an' sit down,' I told him. 'No tricks, or I shoot.'

'Whatever you say, Soledad.' He moved back across the room, still smiling easily, and settled himself in the chair. All the time his dark, piercing eyes studied me carefully. 'What was it you had in mind?'

'Hands on the desk, Jim.' I took a

pace forward from the doorway, the gun levelled on him. 'I came back here to take you in, Mr Treharne. Burrell told me all of it, out in the brush yonder. You're the feller runnin' the whole crooked business, an' it's due to end now. You're goin' back to Tylerville to stand trial, an' I'm takin' you there.'

He laughed at that, lolling back in the chair and shaking his head. By now he'd brushed off most of the mud, and looked neater than ever. And I tell you, that man was handsome enough to stop a railroad train just by looking it in the eye.

'Sure admire your nerve, Soledad,' Treharne said. His gaze touched on me, burning hot. 'Always did admire you, you know that. How do you aim to get out of here?'

'Same way I came in,' I told him.

Outside came a sudden noise of hooves and gunshots and yelling voices, and a bunch of men pushed out on to the street. We watched through the window as a crowd of miners came out of the saloon, guns and carbines in their hands. Four or five unarmed gunmen stumbled ahead of them, their hands tied. A moment later I saw Mulgrew's posse come storming down the street, heading towards us.

'It's over here, Jim,' I told him. 'You're finished in Walleye, or anyplace else. Any minute now your gunhawks will quit, an' Mulgrew will be in here to put the cuffs on you.'

'Seems you're right,' Jim Treharne said. He smiled again, more ruefully than before. 'A pity, Soledad. Together, the two of us could have been quite a team.'

'Yeah, I thought about that too,' I told him. Somehow I couldn't keep the hurt out of my voice. 'Jim, you had everything. Hotel in St Louis, an' Alice, too. Where the hell did you go so wrong?'

'Maybe I don't like to be hobbled too close,' he shrugged, listening as the last of the yells and gunshots died away. Jim Treharne met my look steadily, not smiling for once. 'I had debts I couldn't meet, and I worked out how to get rich without lifting a hand. You need to hear any more?'

'Guess not.' My mind went back to another, earlier time in Walleye, and this time I managed a faint smile of my own. 'How 'bout the grey horse? You still got him?'

'He's tied up out front, on the street.' Treharne glanced through the window as he spoke, that lost look on his face. 'I aimed to teach him some manners later. Now, it don't look like I'll get the chance.'

'Just as well, I'd say.' I flipped the gunbarrel upward, signalling him to rise. 'OK, Jim, let's go. I reckon Mulgrew's gonna be waitin'.'

He was getting up from the chair when a board creaked behind me and I started to turn around. The click of the gun-hammer froze me halfway through the move.

'Stay put, you bitch,' Salinas told me. 'An' throw that pistol down.'

Sound of that chilling voice was the worst thing I'd heard so far. The minute he spoke, I felt my heart stop and my stomach drop away, and for a while I wondered if I was going to need the slop pail in a hurry. I threw the .44 Remington out across the room, and Jim Treharne grinned, scrambling over to pick it off the floor.

'Now stay smart, an' don't move.' From the sound, I worked out he wasn't up close, but standing back a couple of paces beyond the open doorway. Too far for me to jump. 'Saw you ride in, an' come after you through the window. Guess you ain't as sharp as you think.' He pitched his voice a little louder, aiming at Treharne. 'Game's over here, boss, but we kin still git clear. You want her dead?'

'Let her be, Salinas.' Treharne studied me slowly with those dark eyes of his. 'She'll be no trouble without the gun.'

'Maybe so.' The undersized killer thought about that, not sounding too sure. 'Way I see it, she's trouble any time. Reckon I might just finish the job anyway.'

The back hair came up on my neck, and I figured it could be a problem which way I'd empty my guts the fastest, when a tall black-garbed shape loomed up at the window, and I saw the pistol rising for the shot. A moment later the glass shattered, its fragments scattering across the floor, and a bullet thudded into the frame of the door behind me. I was down before the glass broke, hearing Salinas as he swore and fired back. The little gunhawk was inside the doorway now, leaning forward as he lined to shoot again. I kicked the door shut, hearing it slam on his arm, pinned it there with both feet as he yelled and struggled to get free. Across the room Jim Treharne laughed and shook his head, making for the door.

'Sure underestimated you, didn't I?' Treharne said. He gave me a parting wave. '*Adios*, Soledad!'

He tugged the door open and dived outside for the street, just as Reverend Reuben Hall stepped in through the shattered window, pistol in hand. The bearded preacher let him run, hurrying over to where I fought to keep the door shut as Salinas yelled and tried to force it back open. The gun-hand poked through our side, the weapon still in its grip. The reverend whacked his gunbarrel on the wrist, and Salinas yelled harder, the hand opening to let the pistol fall. I slid clear, kicking it away as the preacher dragged the door open and hauled the little gunman inside. Salinas was still struggling to get away when the holy man struck the gun-butt on the smaller man's skull, denting in his hat. Salinas sighed and crumpled up, collapsing to the floor.

'A weak spirit, walking in darkness,' the reverend said. He lowered the gun he held, glancing at me with concern in his eyes. 'You are not hurt, I hope?'

'I'm just fine,' I told him. 'Thanks, Reverend. He'd have killed me for sure.' I picked up the pistol Salinas had dropped, and headed for the door. 'Let's find Treharne!'

'He won't get far,' the reverend called out after me, following. 'We just broke up his gang between us. Those who didn't run are all in custody by now.'

I was out through the door before he finished talking, looking for Treharne. I didn't have far to look. He had the big silver-grey stallion loose from the hitch-rail and was climbing into the saddle, while the horse shrilled and fought against the rein.

'Come back here!' I shouted. I had the pistol levelled on him in the moment he swung the horse from the rail, and from there I don't reckon I could have missed. But when it came to pressing the trigger, my finger wouldn't move. All I could do was watch.

Halfway along the street that grey horse bucked and hunched its back, jumping stiff-legged in the mud.

Treharne lost the rein just before it stopped short again, shooting him out over its bent neck for the street. I heard the noise as he landed, and it turned me sick. The horse took off running, but this time Jim Treharne didn't move.

Seemed like the street was full of people now, the shooting over. Mulgrew and Meredith's miners had the gun-hawks roped, and now they stood staring at the figure of Treharne lying in the dirt. I started running, but Alice was there before me, and when I saw her kneeling by him I stood off and watched. He'd been her husband, after all.

'Jim!' Alice was crying, the tears smearing her face as she sobbed and shook him. 'Jim, honey, talk to me! You know I love you, Jim! I thought you loved me too. Please, Jim, talk to me!'

She broke down, collapsing on him as those sobs shook her body. From the far side Reverend Hall bent over her, murmuring something in a low voice as he tried to calm her down. To me it seemed like it came from a way off, and I was someplace else. I looked down over Alice's heaving shoulder, into the face of Jim Treharne.

At first sight he hardly looked any different. Just as handsome as he'd always been, with those dark eyes staring up into mine. They had a new, surprised kind of expression to them, as if he hadn't been expecting to see me standing there. But I knew he couldn't see me, and the wry tilt of his neck was enough to tell me how he'd died. Jim Treharne wasn't here any more. Only hours back he'd been kissing and hugging me close, and if things had worked out otherwise we might have been closer yet. Minutes ago he'd been as alive as a man could be, grinning as he ducked out through the door. Now that life had left him. No fire in the blood, no light in those eyes. Whatever had been Jim had pulled up stakes and quit, and I wouldn't be seeing him again.

I knew I'd be a while forgetting him. If I ever did.

I was still standing there looking down at him when the dawn broke in the east, and the fierce sun blistered the badlands outside the town.

10

'So that's all, huh?' Finn Mahoney asked.

He leaned across the ragged bar top, his big brown hands a lighter shade against the wood, and studied me with his piercing green eyes. Far side of the bar, I sank my beer to halfway down the glass and nodded, savouring the taste.

'Looks like it, Finn,' I said. 'The gang's cleaned out of Walleye, an' the folks there are back to runnin' the place. Burrell, Hildreth an' Simmons, Ashman an' Brocklehurst are over at the jail-house, waitin' on Judge Garrison. Salinas an' his gunhawks are headed back to El Paso, seems like the Texas Rangers have warrants for most of 'em.'

'An' they gave you back your money,' Finn reminded me. Gangs and gunmen were all very well, but money was money, and Finn liked to keep his priorities right.

'Sure did.' I patted the thick billfold in my back pocket like a long-lost friend. 'Got my pocket pistol back with it, an' the roan horse is out by the rail. Not only that, Mulgrew figures I'm due a cut from the reward money for Salinas an' the rest. Me and Alice an' the reverend, that is. Might take a while to come through, mind, but he claims he'll make sure I get it.'

'You reckon he will?' the redheaded saloonman wanted to know.

'Sure he will,' I told him. 'Mulgrew is straight enough. A mite crusty, is all.'

'He better, the old buzzard,' Finn said. He eyed me thoughtfully, a sharper light in his jade-coloured eyes. 'How about Alice an' the reverend, Soledad? What're they doin' now?'

I took another sip at the beer, trying not to grin too much. Somehow I didn't think it was the reverend's health that he was interested in.

'The reverend's still in Walleye.' I let

the cool beer go down slowly, making it last. 'He aims to settle there, work as a blacksmith while he preaches at the miners every once in a while. 'Walleye shall see the light', that's what he says anyhow.'

'Uhuh.' Finn tried to sound interested, and didn't make it. 'What about Alice?'

'She's in Walleye too,' I said. I peered at him over the rim of my glass, smiling a little as the beer went down. 'Right now, she's still to make up her mind.'

I let my glance drift back towards the doors, and the growing light beyond them. This early, Finn's saloon was pretty quiet, a handful of drinkers nursing their glasses at the tables near the bar. Derby hat and his Mexican sidekick had still to arrive, for which I was mighty thankful. Then again, I wasn't really here in my mind, not this minute. I was recalling Alice, and how she'd made time to corner me alone before I rode out of Walleye and back to Tylerville.

'He's asked me to marry him, Soledad,' Alice told me. Her face was lit up like she was a young kid with her first beau, and she blushed rosier than ever as she spoke. 'He says Walleye could be a fine place to live once it's cleaned up a little, and he'd appreciate it if I chose to settle with him.' She probed at me with her wide blue eyes, still smiling. 'Soledad, what do you think I ought to do?'

'Well, now.' To myself I figured that Walleye could stand a considerable amount more cleaning up than they'd given it so far, but I wasn't about to say it. Not with her so excited and all. 'What'd you tell him, anyhow?'

'I thanked him for his offer, and told him I'd give it serious thought,' Alice said.

'Just what is it you want, Alice?'

'I'm not sure, Soledad.' For the first time I had her frowning, thinking it over. 'It's all been so fast, after all. First Jim was dead, then he turned up alive again, and now . . . ' She sighed, the sadness coming back into her face. 'Some folks would say it was sudden, I suppose.'

'When did you ever care what some folk said?' I wanted to know. Then, more seriously, 'You reckon you'd settle to be a blacksmith's wife, Alice?'

'I might go into business on my own account.' All at once she was bright again, the determined smile coming back. 'The saloon in Walleye is going cheap, and I've a little money saved. And if the reward comes through, as the sheriff promised, I might just take it on.'

'Reverend ain't gonna like that,' I told her, and she shrugged her shoulders.

'Well,' Alice said. 'Maybe I'll marry him and maybe not, but if I do he's going to have to take me as I am.'

'An' he'll be a fool if he ain't mighty glad to do it,' I said. This time I couldn't hide the grin. 'That's what I like to hear, Alice.'

'Why, thank you kindly, Soledad,' she

said in her schoolmarm voice, then burst into a fit of the giggles. Once she calmed down she looked at me, questioningly. 'You will stay for a while, won't you?'

'Sorry, Alice, I can't do that,' I told her. 'That horse herd in Arizona is waitin' on me, an' I already been here five days too long.' Seeing her downcast look, I smiled again. 'An' whether you do or whether you don't, you know I'm gonna wish you all the luck in the world.'

'Oh, Soledad.' She caught hold of me and hugged me like she was about to squeeze me out of breath. 'I shall miss you. You've been a real friend to me. I don't know what I'd have done without you!'

'If you hadn't showed up at the jail, they'd have hanged me for a horse-thief,' I reminded her. 'Seems to me you've been a pretty good friend yourself.'

'I don't believe I ever met anyone like you before.'

'Goes for me too, Alice.'

So we hugged and kissed and said our goodbyes, and Alice cried some. And if there was a little water in my eyes too, what the hell business is it of yours, anyhow?

Trouble with remembering the good times is, after a while you start to recall the bad. I was thinking on Jim Treharne, and brooding some, when Finn's voice pulled me out of my dream.

'You OK, Soledad?' His voice was anxious. 'You look like you seen a ghost.'

'Maybe I did, at that.' I drank the last of my beer and let it settle, studying the flecks of foam in the glass. 'Your place still serves the best in Tylerville, Finn. I have to give you that. How about that business of the fire at Hildreth's? They ever find anyone?'

'Not a trace.' His broad features cracked in a grin. 'Don't reckon they ever will. An' now Hildreth's behind bars, he ain't gonna trouble us over-much.' He stroked his jaw, a mite carefully I thought. 'Bruise is almost healed. Should be able to manage steak an' potatoes in a while.'

'Yeah.' I grinned with him, thinking back. 'Tylerville's gonna be a better place, I reckon. Only don't take it personal if I don't call back for a while, Finn. Last time I rode in they had the rope round my neck.'

'Always good to see you, Soledad. You know that.'

'Sure, Finn. Nice talkin' to you.' I straightened up, and pushed away from the bar. 'I have to be goin' now. Best I should start early, that sun's gonna be hot as hell once it gets up.'

I waved a hand and left him, making my way past the drinkers for the doors.

The roan horse was waiting out by the rail. I'd watered him and fed him a little grain when I brought him from the stables, and now he was eager to go. That horse was sure pleased to see me, and I reckon I felt the same. Give me horses or folks, I'll take horses every time. Once in a while you'll get a mean one, like that big grey was, but mostly you can trust them with your life. More than most folks I know.

'Let's go, feller,' I said. I patted his neck and let him nuzzle my shoulder as I loosened his rope from the rail. 'You an' me got some miles to cover come sundown.'

This business in Tylerville and Walleye was over now, and I had the memories. Some of them I reckon I could have done without, but that ain't the way it works. It had taken five days out of my life, and I was going home with what I'd expected, but I guess I wouldn't have changed it anyhow. Not much comes free nowadays. I'd learned plenty since I rode into Tylerville, and I reckon you have to pay for what you learn.

I climbed into the saddle and started riding.

Other titles in the
Linford Western Library:

A TOWN CALLED
TROUBLESOME

John Dyson

Matt Matthews had carved his ranch out of the wild Wyoming frontier. But he had his troubles. The big blow of '86 was catastrophic, with dead beeves littering the plains, and the oncoming winter presaged worse. On top of this, a gang of desperadoes had moved into the Snake River valley, killing, raping and rustling. All Matt can do is to take on the killers single-handed. But will he escape the hail of lead?